welcome!
browse, sit awhile or borrow.
but, please
RETURN TO:

A RANGER'S TALE

Jacks' Vendetta

**A Novel by
Myron Ferdig**

Dedicated to:

All Those Readers

Who Still Enjoy Picking Up

A Paperback Novel

now and then...

& Especially

If it's a Western!

Other Books by Myron Ferdig

- *A Lad From Sardinia*

  the ADVentures of MorGAN HARMony

  **A High Seas Adventure in The Mediterranean Sea
  in the 1600, story set in prose poetry
  ISBN 978-0-9966042-0-8**

- *Poetpourri*

  A LABγrinth of WANDering Thought

  **A collection of Short Stories, Poems and Prose
  Poetry -- from the Ridiculous to the Sublime.
  ISBN 978-0-9966042-1-5**

This book
is a work of fiction.

Names, characters, events, places or incidents
are the product of the author's imagination
or are used fictitiously,
and -
with the exception of the preface
which is essentially factual
and common knowledge
to any Texas history buff -
any resemblance to actual persons,
living or dead, or to events or locales,
is entirely coincidental.

Preface

Before 1820 most of what is now known as Texas was part of Spain. A fellow by the name of Moses Austin had secured approval from Spain to settle a massive land area in what was then called Tejas. (Teh´hass) His goal was to bring in three hundred immigrant families [history calls them "the Old 300"] to settle the area around the Brazos, San Bernard and Colorado Rivers.

But, things changed. Between 1820 and 1824 Mexico won its independence from Spain. Moses Austin died in 1821, but his son, Steven F. Austin inherited the land grant, and with certain conditions -- newcomers must learn the Mexican language, become citizens and accept the Catholic faith -- approval was received from the new Mexican Regime; he proceeded to bring families into Tejas, to fulfill his father's dream. These first legitimate immigrants were called Texians. The population grew exponentially, and in just three years' time it reached almost two thousand.

The Mexican government told Austin that protection against the influx of the criminal element flowing in from Kansas, Oklahoma and elsewhere, and the native marauders {especially Comanche and Kiowa} was entirely on his shoulders; Mexico wouldn't intercede.

In 1823, Austin hired ten men to act as a "Ranging" Police Force to protect his Texian residents from Indians and criminals, and to keep the peace in his "experimental colonies" -- thus, the legend of the Texas Rangers began.

By the end of 1835, the Texas Rangers had grown to become an official "Republic of Texas" force of over sixty men, made up of three divisions, and took part in the fight for independence against Mexico.

In March of 1836, Tejas declared itself an independent republic. There were fewer than eight thousand Mexicans now residing in this rough, unforgiving terrain, but over four times as many immigrants -- mostly U.S. citizens.

By this time, the Rangers were a hardened fighting force. They had earned a reputation that approached legendary among the citizenry, the Mexicans and the Indians. They received nationwide fame in the U.S. press, as news of their exploits, whether true or exaggerated, became widespread, effectively establishing the Rangers as part of American folklore.

This is one such tale

I, once again thank my wife,
Darlene
For the hours she spent
questioning my destruction of the
English language with such words as
"mebbe", "shudda", sumthin' and
"cuz".
Through it all, with her
teacher's mind and gritted teeth,
she still managed to brave the
elements to edit my story
brilliantly.

A
RANGER'S
TALE

Jacks' Vendetta

Chapter 1

Brisbie, Texas
Early FridayMorning
June 26, 1840

Witherspoon pulled his second boot on, tucked his favorite green and white checkered shirt into his pants, buckled his colt-holstered belt around his 34" waist and headed for the door.

"Ain't you forgettin' somethin', cowboy?"

He turned to the smiling brunette on the pillow. In mock drudgery, he tossed a coin on the bed beside her.

"Been married to you for six years, Lottie, and you still demand payment for havin' the pleasure of my company."

"Your company, Jeb Witherspoon? You've taken advantage of my delicacies for all these years and still lack the proper appreciation; but I'll forgive you again if you come over here and give me a kiss before you walk out that door."

"Is this goin' to cost me another silver?"

"You bet your skinny ass!" Lottie smiled. She sat up on one elbow as he slid his left arm around her neck.

"And don't you go pokin' my eye out with that big ol' star on your shirt!"

He dropped the silver piece down her gaping night shirt.

"For our retirement then," he quipped, as his right hand tried to follow the coin, only to be jerked away by her lightning-fast free hand.

"Coin only, cowboy. Squire's a'waitin'," she laughed. "Now run along!"

He stood, pulled his hat down firmly to his ears, turned, took one last, lingering look at his delicious bride, tipped his hat brim, mumbled something under his breath, showing her another wistful face-full of disappointment, and pulled the door open.

Sun was just about ready to poke its nose over *Mt. Daggett*. Jeb shut the door softly behind him, yawned, stretched his 6'5" frame, tightening every muscle from toe to finger tips, and thanked the Good Lord for another day.

"Star, hell!" he muttered aloud, -- but only to himself. Texas Rangers haven't got the money for real stars, he mused; just a five-sided star printed on a piece of official-looking paper, and signed by Steven Austin back in 1836. Jeb kept his in his vest pocket at all times for identification.

He and Squire decided long ago to make their own stars out of Mexican Pesos. Had old man Dutch Cairns, the blacksmith in Wichita Falls, fashion ten of them, patterned after the picture on the letter --

had them inscribed, too, all around the circle --

Cost $2.30 for the star with the pin on the back, and an extra $2.00 for the inscribing.

Someday soon this Republic will be rich enough to make up some stars for us boys who are keeping the citizens safe, he thought to himself, but for now, we do just fine. He made his way down the worn oak planks of the walkway. Someday soon, he mused, "Hell, they's always a someday."

The front of the *Good Night Hotel* was shaded by a long veranda held up by three ornate, white columns. Hitching rails, in turn, were fastened to these support columns, and this morning it seemed all the ponies in Northeast Texas were tied to these rails.

"Hmmph! This must have been a good night for the *Good Night*," he spoke aloud, then turned to left and right to see if there were any who heard. But the street was empty in the early dawn, so smiling to himself he ducked beneath a rail and pushed his way between a couple of saddle-weary sorrels, noting they had just recently been ridden. Patting their wet, quivering flanks as he strode by, he stepped off the boardwalk, and counted nine more ponies, still saddled, tied along the rail, wet with sweat.

A few curiously disturbing thoughts flashed through his mind: Who just rode into Brisbie in such a hurry? Why were there four different brands on the rumps of the only four of the nine which were branded, since they'd obviously come in together? One brand was vaguely familiar -- he couldn't really place it -- and he recognized none of the others - so, just where were these strangers from? And lastly, since it was just barely dawn, and most of these nags had surely been ridden long and hard, what was the big hurry to ride through the night?

So before he crossed the dusty main street toward *The Copperhead*, one of the many Brisbie waterholes, the Ranger retraced his steps to the hotel's lobby, where Frank Knight smiled up at him as he pushed open the door and approached the check-in desk.

"Comin' in for breakfast, Jeb? Where's Lottie?"

"Howdy, Frank. No, Just a question. I see a few horses tied up outside. Been rode hard. You servin' some strangers this mornin'? Looks like quite a bunch -- mebbe seven, eight, nine from the look of it."

"Matter of fact, yes. Dusty bunch. Rented one of our bunkhouse rooms for tonight. They're in the washhouse right now, cleanin' up a bit. Said they'd be in here for some grub shortly. Claim to be down from Nor-east of here, headin' fer some feller's ranch out New Mexico Territory after a day's stop-over here. A fella called Jacks signed in for the whole bunch."

"Hmmph! New Mexico, eh? Thanks, Frank." Jeb again retraced his steps, closing the hotel door softly behind him, and pondering the Jacks' boys, he made his way to *The Copperhead.*

Squire and some others were already there, including that new fellow, Drummer, enjoying a cup, waiting for him and the remainder of the expected lawmen; should be quite a powwow, he mused. Smiling and raising an arm in greeting, Ranger Jacob 'Jeb' Witherspoon stooped his lanky frame low through the door and entered.

George Birdwell, sitting at the head of the long table, only grunted an abbreviated greeting as Witherspoon ambled in. Pulling out a plush-bottomed wooden chair, Jeb slid in between Drummer and Squire, tipped an empty mug right-side up, and poured himself a coffee from the steaming pot in the center. He offered a refill to all those seated, placed the pot back on the hot pad, then leaned back, sipping the strong, freshly brewed eye-opener. He listened to the small talk going around the table, and as usual, he had a few things to say as well.

"Anyone here ride into town through the night?"

"Hell no, Jeb. I rode in yestiday, along with George," Harlan drawled. An' I saw this young feller," pointing to Drummer, "draggin' his saddle off'n that big buckskin over at the livery stable early last evenin'. An' Squire, you stayed upstairs here -- didn'ya, Squire? Why you askin', Jeb?"

Everyone at the table figured Witherspoon was about to come out with a typical "Witherspoon witticism", but he remained sober.

"I counted ten or eleven nags tied up at Knight's place, still frothin' at the bit, when I started over here. Didn't recognize any brands. Curious."

"Shall we take a walk over there and do some checkin'?" This time it was Harlan Franklin who spoke.

Birdwell answered for them all. "Later. We have some business to attend!"

Chapter 2

George Birdwell was edgy. All morning his mind had been pacing an imaginary floor. Breakfast should have been out of the way by this time, and the meeting well underway; but still missing were John and Henry Wortham, the two brothers out of Plainview; Martin Fredericks from out Lubbock way hadn't shown up either. He decided he could wait no longer.

"Gents," he said, "let's make sure everyone here knows everyone else, then let's have some breakfast and get this conference started. We'll take a gander across the street after."

Introductions all around: Harlan Franklin, Curt O'Brien and Benson Hawks from north and west of the Trinity; Jimmy Hanks along with Simon Ellsworth from the area between Midland and Abilene; and of course, Squire Daniels and Jeb Witherspoon, peacekeepers from the Oklahoma Territory all across north Texas from the Red River to Wichita Falls, and going all the way up the panhandle north and west of Amarillo.

"Alright now, before we have our powwow and swearing-in ceremony for Drummer, here," said George, "we'll have breakfast, bought by the great Republic of Texas!" He motioned for the waitress. "Gentlemen, let's eat! Steak and eggs for everyone."

"Amen!" Jeb said, drowned out by a chorus of "Alright!" and "Yahoo!" from the rest of the lawmen.

Alice appeared from the kitchen, carrying a dozen plates, which were quickly spread around, and from her apron pocket she produced the usual cutlery. Then she disappeared, to reappear once more carrying a huge platter -- man-sized chunks of Texas beef, piled high. After two or three more trips from the kitchen with her production of eggs, beans, and sourdough biscuits, Alice was happy -- as were all participants -- with the morning's feast. Half an hour later, she cleared the table, brought out more steaming coffee, and finally disappeared into the kitchen for the last time. She went about her clean-up chores while this satisfied, fledgling group of Texas law-keepers sat, intent now, upon George Birdwell.

"You all know by now, gents, there's a lot of politicking going on. Houston's been replaced by Lamar, so the fight for statehood goes on; Houston's pressing for statehood. I believe he's back in Washington this very moment, while Lamar -- well he's gone to Britain and France and some other places in Europe. He's already received official recognition for the Republic of Texas as an independent nation over there, and now he's trying to set up financial stability by putting some trade agreements together. You've no doubt seen the

Redbacks floating around, haven't you? Probably already had a few cross your palm. The Texas dollar, my friends! And that, too, is Lamar's doing. He's moving the capitol from down south in Houston to central Texas, at Waterloo. You aware of that? He's petitioned to rename it Austin after the man. That means we'll have a Texas Ranger outpost in north-central Texas before long."

News to most around the table. Some didn't even know who Lamar was. So, Birdwell went through the credentials of Col. Mirabeau B. Lamar.

"He distinguished himself for bravery by rescuing two soldiers single-handedly from the Mexicans at the Battle of San Jacinto, even to the point that the Mexicans saluted his courage; he's now our President, nominated and elected into office in December of 1838, defeating Houston. I think Austin could have beat him, but the unfortunate demise of Austin left a big, gaping hole in worthy competition."

"Oh, I almost forgot! Alice! Bring out that covered trolley!"

"What, George? Texas buyin' dessert, too? drawled Harlan.

"Naw. Got a surprise for you fellows. The best present you'll ever get from the Republic. Austin had his eye on them before he died," George continued, as Alice brought a mounded table cloth-covered trolley from the kitchen and pushed it next to Birdwell. He lifted the cloth to expose twenty identical wooden boxes, each one stamped, *Colt Patterson #5.*

"Boys, pass these around 'til each one of you has two boxes. Jeb, Squire, you already have one, so just take one box. Okay, now. open your box."

George continued: "Now, they're all the same, so you boys need only open one box each right now. This fellow, Colt invented a repeating revolver back east somewhere -- shoots five shots before it needs reloading. He thought he had a big contract with the U.S. Army -- sent them out a thousand of these as a trial, but the cavalry nixed it. So he turned around and offered them to Texas. Austin had already told some of the boys about them, so as soon as Jack Hayes became Ranger boss down in Houston, he saw them and snapped up a hundred and eighty revolvers and a like amount of rifles to outfit all of us. They'd been sitting in a Texas surplus warehouse until now. I brought a few of the rifles along with me, but not enough for everyone here. They shoot eight shots before they need reloading."

"Eight shots? Hell, I'll take one!" Harlan broke in.

"Me, too, if it shoots true! I've just got Mildred to shoot what I aim at, and it took me three years to get her trained up good!" O'Brien quipped, to a few smiles.

Same question buzzed around the room as Birdwell motioned for Alice to bring out a rifle for inspection.

"I brought four. They will go to. "

Just then a youngster of about sixteen pushed open the door. Birdwell stopped in mid-sentence and looked at the boy quizzically.

"Can we help you, Son?"

"No, sir. I'm looking for my sister, Carrie, but I don't see her in here, so I'll be going." And he was gone.

George frowning, continued, "They will go to those who have served the longest. Jeb, you and Squire, one each. John Wortham was supposed to get one, but he isn't here, so the other two will go to Jimmy Hanks and Curt O'Brien. Now all of us will get ours later. And," turning to the four new owners, "if you fellows don't like them, don't be bashful. Let us know. We need to field test them to be satisfied, so keep your old gear."

"Now, getting back to Lamar, he has some good ideas and some really bad ones. You know for yourself, we had two Indian Ranger outfits -- good men. Hell, I recruited most of them myself, and even fought against the Comanche with them. Well, old Lamar comes along and says to get rid of them. He hates all Indians, and has ordered them all removed from within Texas boundaries, even our own Ranger boys!"

"You gonna go along with'im, Sir?" asked one at the table. "Don't seem right."

"Well, I suppose. I have my orders, and orders are orders; but in my mind, it would be one hell of a lot better to keep these fellows by our side. Sure, the Comanche and Kiowa are ruthless critters, but they seem to be always fighting somebody, whether it be Texians, Mexicans or their own kind. This last order from Lamar will sure stir the pot!"

"What other piece of bad news you got for us, George?" O'Brien asked, shaking his head at the confirmation of the scuttlebutt they'd been hearing out of Houston.

"You know Simon Taylor got himself a pretty little wife from the Coushatta tribe; four, five kids, too. They gonna have to get packed up and go, too?"

"No. Not at all. Lamar wrote and signed an exclusive treaty with them last year, so Lt. Taylor's off the hook."

"Should have done the same with our Ranger boys," Jeb concluded, to some nods and grunts of agreement from around the table.

"Going on, gents, with the last bit I have to share, and it's not all bad. We've been a rag-tag group at best until now, but under the new Rangers' administration, Hayes says we've been assured of wages retroactive to your signing on.

We'll still need to provide our own horse and weapons, Colt weaponry aside, wages are $20.00 per month, guaranteed. $5.00 dollars in hand, and $15.00 paid out in property anywhere in Texas. We just go to any county seat and sign out a deed with the agency, and that will assure you the property is yours. We've grown from about forty men to somewhere near one hundred fifty just in the last year, and we've only lost a handful of Rangers since this new ruling has come into effect, so if you have your heart set on a piece of ground, stake it out soon."

"How do we get the 'in hand' money, George?"

"Yeah, explain this retroactive stuff."

So George went through the details with each one, and gave silver coins, minted by the U.S. government to assure correct silver content -- each $20.00 piece worth four months' prior service. In addition, each Ranger was handed two papers signed by Captain John Coffee Hayes. The first paper to be shown to recording clerks in county seats as to the validity of land parcel deeds; the second to take to a local bank to draw the $5.00

monthly fee for service. The bank would keep a tally, of course, and be reimbursed from the coffers of the Texas Ranger organization.

"Now, Drummer!" Birdwell got to his feet, and faced the youngest man at the table.

"Yes, Sir!" Drummer stood.

"What's your Christian name, Son?"

"Drummer Hawkins, Sir"

"No, not your nickname, Son, your given name," Birdwell muttered, looking up at the slim young giant facing him.

"Not a nickname. My grandpa was a drummer in the war, Sir. My ma gave me that name, Sir."

"Well, I be damned! OK then, how old are you, Drummer Hawkins?

"Twenty-seven, Sir." An' I'm good with a pistol, rifle and horses -- and a good tracker! I read and write pretty good, I keep my mouth shut so I don't get into uncalled-for trouble, an' I ain't married."

"Somebody vouch for all the merits I've just heard?" George turned to the others in the room.

"Carries a smooth-bore shotgun, and hits what he aims at," Squire attested. "As he says, good tracker, too. Not too long ago, only three of us -- we tracked nine outlaws, Curly Beecher's bunch. Had them all buried up at Red Rock. At the time, of course, he wasn't a Ranger, but he acted like a Ranger -- carried himself well. He ain't married. Don't even think he has a girl."

"We'll, that's cuz he keeps his mouth shut," Witherspoon chimed in, to a roar of laughter.

Alice poked her head from the kitchen doorway and chimed in, "I'll take him. I can use someone to help me cook and wait on my customers, clean up the place and keep his mouth shut. And he's not married! That's a great deal!"

While everyone guffawed, poor Drummer's face became as red as the checkered table cloths; his shoulders slouched a bit, but he stood, stupid grin on his face, eyes focused on George.
"Afraid not, Alice. The Texas Rangers have the first crack at him."

"Drummer Hawkins, raise your right hand."

Once done, Birdwell summed up:

"Gents, thanks for coming today. I, myself believe statehood's inevitable. We're bound to join up with the Union sooner or later. There's those who will fight until the last dog is hung for recognition as a separate Republic, while here we are, just trying to keep Texas safe. Let's do our jobs with pride. Texas needs us!"

"One more thing, George," Squire spoke up. "Jeb and I had some badges made up by the smithy over in Wichita Falls. They look like this," and he opened his long coat to expose the star on his vest. "Not enough for everyone here, but with your permission, I'm giving one to Drummer since he's riding along with Jeb and me, and the others I'll give to you."

"Absolutely, Squire. Looks like some mighty fine work. What did they cost? And where'd you get the silver?"

Jeb spoke then, "Cost Squire an' me sixteen Mexican pesos, that's eight apiece; then it cost me one unpleasant night when Lottie found out I spent some hard-earned retirement money. But I should have a very pleasant night tonight when I hand her the back pay."

Ripples of laughter and broad smiles flooded the room.

"There was a fella down in Houston who made up some for a few Rangers," continued Birdwell, "and another gent who fashioned some from pesos as well; but his were six-pointed, and neither were as well made as these. They look just like the Texas Seal. Thanks!"

"They do, indeed. That was the idea. And, you are welcome, Sir," drawled Witherspoon.

So the little convention, complete with swearing-in ceremony, was over; all seemed satisfied with the arrangement. George Birdwell went into the kitchen to settle up with Alice, Jimmy Hanks and Harlan Franklin went upstairs to gather up their belongs for their journey home, while Squire, Witherspoon and the newest Ranger walked through the saloon swinging doors -- determined to find the Jacks' riders from last night's ride, and discover why they had been in such a hurry. But, strange! No horses were in sight. They trotted across the street to the *Good Night.* Squire opened the front door. Neither Suzanna nor her father stood behind the desk. Hmmph! That was strange, indeed! He called up the winding stairway, "Anybody home?" but the hotel echoed back only an eerie emptiness. Frowning, he stepped back outside, where his comrades were waiting on the boardwalk.

"Seems no one around. Mighty peculiar!"

"Lottie!" Witherspoon raced around the corner of the boardwalk to the entry into his hotel room, Drummer and Squire on his heels. Empty! The room showed signs of a struggle: wash basin and doilies from the dresser were on the floor. On the bed, broken, lay the pitcher, still dripping water to the floor. Mixed in and turning the puddle reddish was blood!

"Son of a Bitch! Son of a Bitch! Son of a Bitch! You bastards! You're dead! You hear me, Jacks? You're dead!"

While Jeb was bellowing, overwhelmed with the shock and pain of the vision set before him, Squire quietly said, "Drummer, go fetch our horses!"

Chapter 3

Squire raised his new rifle to the sky and squeezed off three rounds. Folks came running from all over town at the distress signal, including the other Rangers, Brisbie sheriff, Tom Lewis and some hands from the Double Bar S ranch outside Brisbie, who were in town for supplies.

"What the hell happened, Witherspoon?" Lewis asked his friend, who by this time was in the saddle, straddling his big white mare, ready to throw the spurs to her haunches.

"They took Lottie! That's what happened, Tom. They took my Lottie!"

"Sheriff! Around back!" came a call from one of the townfolk. "It's old man Knight!"

George Birdwell yelled, "Hold up a minute, Witherspoon!" He, Lewis, and some others ran in the direction of the voice to find the crumpled remains of the late Frank Knight, proprietor of the *Good Night Hotel,* lying in a pool of blood next to a garbage pile near the back door -- head bashed in and throat slit.

They ran, now, through the back door into the kitchen and on into the small adjacent office -- where Suzanna, Frank Knight's daughter, always kept the hotel receipts and other important *Good Night* papers locked away in a cabinet drawer. That cabinet had been smashed, drawer contents strewn in every direction, and a small, open strongbox lay empty on Suzanna's desk. From the kitchen came yet another cry of outrage and dismay.

"It's that young half-breed kid, Tinato. You know -- Timmy. The one Suzanna hired on as a dish washer. Pool of blood in front of broom closet. Found him in there. Been scalped. Got a note stuck to his chest with an ice pick. Says 'thanks fer brekfist.' Ain't no sign of Suzanna!"

Sheriff Lewis wheeled and stared hard at Birdwell.

"What's goin' on here, George? Waltz right into our town, plenty of lawmen around, then waltz right on back outta here, after torturing and robbing, killing a prominent citizen and looks like even kidnapping two ladies! Broad daylight, it is! Damn!"

They walked back through the front door of the hotel to find Witherspoon almost fit to be tied with rage.

"They already got hours on us, George. We gotta go! Least-ways I gotta! My whole life's tied on the back of some nag, being dragged to who knows where, and you say, 'just a minute'? I ain't waitin' no longer! Jacks is mine!" And with that, the big white mare, ears flattened, flanks smarting from the angry Ranger's quirt, burst up the road, heading northeast out of Brisbie in the logical direction the Jacks' boys would have chosen.

Birdwell watched him for only brief moment, mumbled something about Jacks; turned to his Rangers and asked, "Any of you gents have someplace else you need to be? I must get on over to Abilene for a similar meeting as we had here, but this outrage is Ranger business. Harlan, Jimmy, either of you have pressing business elsewhere?"

"George, Squire, I have a case about as bad as this one down near Lubbock. Only dropped it to be here. Promised I'd be back by tomorrow. Sorry, but I can't stay on here. My best to you and Jeb."

That was Jimmy Hanks; and, one by one the others expressed the need to be elsewhere, which was understood, as this meeting, though necessary, broke their pattern of law enforcement in their own territories. The rush of newcomers to Texas had a way of bringing an increased amount of trouble.

Harlan Franklin, however, wholeheartedly agreed to make the Jacks' situation his own project, and would certainly ride with the other three -- for which he was warmly welcomed.

"I'd like to tag along as well. Don't need no badge to shoot those swine. This is my town, my people!" The voice was that of Wilson Tanner, one of the Double Bar-S boys. In unison came. "Yes, Sir."

"And me, too," piped up Big Kurt Farber, the town blacksmith. "Suzanna, she is a good girl. My friend!"

Sheriff Lewis nodded to Birdwell. "I can deputize them, but my jurisdiction won't mean much if they're too far from Brisbie. Better that you make them temporary Rangers."

"True enough, Tom. You remember that

name, Jacks, from anywhere? It's rollin' around in my head, but can't quite pin it down.... might be just a coincidence, but I'm sure I've heard it before." Before the sheriff gave an answer, George said, "It'll come to me."

He then turned to the two new volunteers, "Wilson and Kurt! Raise your right hands! As extreme circumstances exist, it is of necessity and within my power to enlist the two of you in the pursuit and capture, as you see fit, of this particular band of unworthies now known to us as the 'Jacks' gang'. You are now a part of the Texas militia for the Republic of Texas. Act accordingly! Understand? This post is temporary. You are to take orders from Squire Hawkins, here. Should you wish to continue, Squire will give me a written report as to your acumen and abilities."

Looking at the group, Birdwell waved. "Gentlemen, good hunting."

Chapter 4

North Texas Plains
Friday Mid-Morning
June 26, 1840

Looked like at least nine, or possibly as many as all eleven horses that had been tied in front of the hotel, but Witherspoon couldn't tell for sure. Tracks were plain enough at first, and they were damn sure headed north as he had expected.

He thought aloud, "New Mexico, my ass! Just a band of no-good scum, taking any shyster advantage they can!"

He shook his head at the thought of the young half-Mexican, half-Caddo lad who helped Suzanna every day at the hotel -- dining room chores, cleaning out vacated rooms, running errands; always bright eyes, eager, a toothy smile, learning the language, beaming with delight each time someone noticed and commented on his progress -- and now? "Ahhgh!" He shook his head again.

And Old Man Knight! Wouldn't cheat a soul. Made sure Lottie and I had the best the hotel had to offer in rooms or room service, bottle of my favorite wine at dinner, a special cigar -- or, for Lottie from who knows where -- a wrapped square of chocolate! Hell, the *Good Night* put Brisbie on the map! Most any traveler from Dallas to the Panhandle knew you could never go wrong if you rested your head on a *Good Night* pillow! ... And once again, Witherspoon sighed aloud.

He kept pushing Lottie to the back of his head. He just couldn't bear the thoughts that tried to creep through the dizzying haze and shine bright as the sun; he turned to Suzanna, but that was too close. So he concentrated on the hoof prints that had churned up the ground in front of him, making it easy enough to follow.

The terrain stretching out before him was basic but beautiful: tall grasses, larch-wood, scrub ash and pines dotted the landscape, with an occasional Jacaranda for a blaze of purple color, and the taller Osage Orange -- Bodark, Squire called it. God threw in a few cottontail rabbits and even one white-tail to keep him company as he focused on the lukewarm trail. Witherspoon couldn't help but feel a refreshing coming over him at the beauty that surrounded him. He loved this part of Texas.

Then his mind retraced its steps back to the task at hand. One of the ponies was skittish: tried to prance this way and that -- like a race horse that was reined in to keep from galloping; one of them was riding heavy -- maybe a pack horse -- maybe laden with foodstuffs from the larder of the *Good Night*'s kitchen. Or, maybe the ladies are tied to it, riding double. So his thoughts turned once again to Suzanna.

"Don't you worry none, Suzanna! Be strong! Be brave! Me'n the boys are right behind! Jacks and his crew don't know what a Texas Ranger can do when he's a bit riled! You'll be back behind that counter by the time "

He stopped short. Something caused him to look up from his gaze at the ground, and startled Jeb Witherspoon to his withers. He let out a curse!

"Damn you to hell, Jacks! Damn you to hell!"

In front of him, not thirty yards away stood a tall, stately Osage-Orange. Three friends, all Texas Rangers, were hanging on a low branch of that tree, swinging in the Texas breeze, rope bound and decidedly dead.

Chapter 5

Jeb had just cut the first Ranger down and was cradling his head, when Squire and his other companions rode up.

"John Wortham, his brother's here, too." Jerking his thumb behind him -- "and Marty." Tears welled up in Witherspoon's eyes. He sighed. "Sons'a'bitches."

Squire cursed. "Let's get 'em down and get 'em buried. Drummer, you and Kurt, here dig some graves." He frowned and cursed again. "They couldn't make the meeting. Now we know why."

The holes were deep to keep coyotes and other marauders from finding an easy meal. They lay them as gentle as lawmen knew how, and packed the soil back over them, mounded a bit as a memorial; Squire said a few words about the hereafter, and a bit about seeking righteous vengeance, noting that there is a place for an "eye for an eye", and an unwritten "scalp for a scalp".

"No sign of horses, truck, or any other gear," called out Wilson. "Every one of their shirts been ripped where you might figure a star woulda been pinned. Ain't no stars."

Sure, the ceremony took precious time away from their primary cause, but it had to be done, and done as right as could be. At least, now, John and Henry Wortham, along with Martin Fredericks, Texas Rangers all, were given a proper send-off.

"How far ahead you figure, Drummer?" Witherspoon asked, hoping the young tracker had an extra sense.

"Not sure at this point, Sir. But I figure, unless they head west for higher country, we can make pretty good time and catch up before nightfall. Keep the horses at a slow trot, and if the soil gets any softer, we can get in a half hour or so at a gallop. Lots of daylight, still, and tracking is easy."

"Let's ride, then," said Jeb. "And Drummer!"

"Yes, Sir?"

"Don't call me Sir!"

Chapter 6

Brisbie, Texas
Friday Morning
June 26, 1840

While the Rangers were settling in at *The Copperhead's* table, another scene was shaping up across the street. Jacks and his seven companions, washed up, hair combed, were being served their breakfast as well -- in the *Good Night Hotel* dining parlor. Most of the patrons were either not yet up, or had finished and gone, leaving only one middle-aged gent with a gold watch fob hanging from a vest pocket. The chair beside him was vacant but for a grey garment of some kind, a strange black hat, and a pair of gloves. The gentleman sat at a corner table as the eight walked in from the washhouse.

Rough looking crowd, Suzanna thought to herself as she poured coffee. As she did so, another of their group arrived, a boy no older than sixteen or seventeen, hurried over to Jacks and whispered in his ear. Jacks raised both eyebrows, then furrowed them, motioned the lad to take a place at the table.

There was no menu -- it was always flapjacks, scrambled eggs and thick cuts of side bacon set in the middle of the table -- and as a platter emptied, another piled high, immediately took its place. Conversation was low and at a minimum, she noted. At times one would comment on the gent in the corner and the others would turn and stare.

Breakfast nearly over for the group, they enjoyed a last cup of coffee. As they did so, the gent in the corner got up, smiled at Suzanna.

"Delicious, my dear, as usual. Put it on my tab. I'll settle up when I leave Thursday."

He donned the top hat, the grey cloak, pulled on the riding gloves insuring that each finger found its home, and bid Suzanna adieu with a nod, and, "Until tomorrow morning, my dear," and walked out.

One of the Jacks' crew cackled, "Did you boys ever see a dude wearing a chimney before?"

Uncontrolled laughter burst forth from the table, followed by coughing, choking, faces full of tears, trying to catch breaths; in the midst of which, Jacks whispered something to the red-headed ruffian on his right. That fellow got up, and disappeared, heading for the hotel lobby.

Suzanna was always in charge of breakfast time, and as always, her father stood behind the desk for the check-out duties, as he did this morning.

There was no Mrs. Knight. She had been lost to a sickness when Suzanna was no more than two or three, and Suzanna's memory of her had faded each year. By now, a grown woman of twenty-four, her only memories were those repeated by her father, "She was very smart -- tall and strong. And she was beautiful -- like you."

This particular morning, standing behind the front desk, Frank Knight looked up to see two guests enter from the dining hall: the first, the gentleman in room 27 upstairs, followed moments later by one of the gents in the bunkhouse room around back.

The second fellow began up the winding stairway, taking two treads at a time.

"Hey, young Son! Where you headed? Ain't no need you going upstairs. As I recall, I checked you in early this morning. Mr. Jacks and all of you are quartered in the bunkhouse out around back."

"Yeah." The young redhead nodded, hopping down and ambling to the desk.

"Jacks saw the watch that gent had, and wondered where he bought it, and would he sell it. What room is he in? Jacks won't like it if I don't come back with an answer."

Eyes narrowing, Frank Knight reached for his pistol under the counter. But it was too late. The redhead whipped out his own revolver and slammed the butt into Knight's temple. Then twice more for good measure as the innkeeper slowly crumpled to the floor.

The redhead pored over the register until he found some entries that looked promising:

Room 27.	Arrival	Departure
Mr. Samuel Hardy *Federal Surveyor*	Tues, June 23	Sat. June 27

Scanning the log further, his eye came upon a name that made him stop short to re-read:<u>Room 11.</u>

<u>Name</u>	<u>Arrival</u>	<u>Departure</u>
Witherspoon & wife *Texas Ranger*	Thur. June 25	Fri. June 26

Quickly he grabbed the extra set of keys for the two rooms and, packing the unconscious Frank Knight up the staircase he came face to face with the surveyor.

"Back in your room, Samuel," he demanded, as he dumped Knight's body unceremoniously to the floor, at the same time waving his pistol in the surveyor's face.

The shocked gentleman obediently retraced his steps, turned his key in the latch and entered. He hardly felt the knife blade.

"Crazy Red" as his friends called him, measured off the room for valuables, loot, anything of value, including the gold watch that now hung, doused with blood, from the Federal surveyor's vest. He wiped it carefully with a bed sheet, tucked it in his pocket, and continued his search.

"Oh, looky here! You have a ...." he looked down at Hardy's body, "you *had* a money belt. But now look! Crazy Red's got a money belt!"

The redhead stuffed most of his plunder in a pillow case. The watch and gold chain, of course, he would give to Jacks; but Jacks didn't need to know about the money belt, the emerald ring or gold cuff links. Those were his! To make things look honorable, Crazy Red threw in the pillow case a few pieces of Mexican silver that were on the dresser.

Then he donned the grey cloak and the top

hat, admired himself in the small mirror above the dresser, and quietly exited, locking the door behind him. In the hallway he almost stumbled over Knight's body.

The man was probably already dead from the pistol-whipping, but Crazy Red slit his throat anyway, and, seeing a window at the end of the hallway, he opened it, looked down, saw the pile of rubbish below, and tossed Frank out the window.

Satisfied with his work of horror, back down the spiral staircase he strode, pillow case slung over his new, grey cloak, money belt around his waist -- tucked under his shirt, chimney hat on his head. Crazy Red headed back to the parlor.

Suzanna was sitting in her office chair, that little cubicle adjacent to the dining room where she always sat after the breakfast was served. She had just presented the last order and bill of the morning -- the one for the Jacks' crew -- when she heard a strange "*thwapp!*" sound from outside the back door.

"Timmy, would you go outside and see what that noise is? Sounded like something fell over. Might be cats again or rats, or probably both -- in the rubbish."

"Sure." And out the door he went. Jacks, in the meantime, walked into her office, her private domain, to "settle the bill" as he called it.

"Sorry. Please just sit at your table. I'll be there in a minute," she smiled up at him.

But it happened at that moment Timmy came rushing through the kitchen door, his red face had gone completely white.

"Mr. Frank!" he cried. "Mr. Frank!"

Suzanna, startled and confused, said, "I don't

understand. You mean my pa? Frank Knight?"

Half turning, she caught sight of Crazy Red entering the dining hall, wearing the Federal surveyor's cloak and hat, and knew the *Good Night Hotel* was in dire trouble.

But before Timmy could say another word, a big hand clasped over his mouth. Suzanna looked up at Jacks desperately. He simply smiled and said, "We have ourselves a situation, I'm afraid."

Red came into the cubicle and whispered something in Jacks' ear.

In answer Jacks smiled. "Tie her up and gag her so she can't make a sound. Take her up to the front."

That done, Jacks and his men ransacked the office, taking all the day's receipts and anything else of value, while Timmy watched in horror. Then Jacks scribbled a note: "thanks fer brekfist" and lay it on the desk.

Crazy Red, not satisfied with those niceties, found an ice pick that Suzanna used as a spiked memo holder, pushed the spike through the note, and thrust the ice pick through Timmy's chest. Still not satisfied with his brutality, he proceeded even further -- as the others cringing, exited the parlor in silence.

<div align="center">~~~~~</div>

"So," Jacks turned to his men, "One Ranger, a Jeb Witherspoon slept here last night, eh? Might be gone by now, but let's just pay a visit to Room 11 and see."

"Ain't he one of the Rangers that wiped out Curly Beecher's little band over near Red Rock? I hear tell there was him an' bout ten others. Killed them all! No mercy whatsoever!"

"The very same. And they was twenty of them!" another of Jacks' men said. "Came in Red Rock just a'whoopin' an'a hollerin' about how brave they was."

Jacks just smiled. Every time he'd heard that story there were more lawmen than before.

~~~~~

Room 11 was without Jacob Witherspoon; but there was nonetheless, a very valuable prize. This lady put up one hell of a fight, but in the end, she was overpowered, gagged tightly, wrapped in the room's bedsheets, hustled to the horses where she was tied tightly to the pommel of one of Jacks' spare horses, newly acquired -- courtesy of the Texas Militia. Suzanna was given the same treatment on another pony. The third Ranger pony was laden down with spoils taken from the *Good Night*. With that, the riders mounted and headed out the way they had come.

It was a good morning, Jacks thought. We planned to rob the bank and mebbe kill the local lawman while we were at it, but when Boo came in with news that the town was full of lawmen sitting right across the street drinking coffee, with guns drawn and laying on the table in front of them, well, although it was tempting, the better part of wisdom told him it's best not to walk into a room filled with loaded guns setting on a table. No, the best way is to continue picking them off, one lawman at a time. Robbing the hotel was twice as good anyway. Not only close to $300 in cash receipts, some guests' valuables, a decent, free breakfast for the crew, a
~~~~~

week's foodstuffs, two ladies to keep his boys occupied; but to top it off, ten to fifteen lawmen sitting right across the street while they were looting! A bit more respect and notoriety for his band. Ha! This day marked a day sure to have the Texas Rangers on their trail! So a bit more fun, indeed! And, no other than Jacob "Jeb" Witherspoon would, for sure, be the next Ranger to feel their wrath, what with his wife held captive.

Yessir, indeed! It was a good morning!

Chapter 7

Indian Territory
Friday Mid-Morning
June 26, 1840

Four miles north of their "Hanging Tree", dry ground became damp -- moistened by a little rivulet from one of the many tributaries of the Red River as it followed the slightest slope of the country and found its way onto the roadway Jacks and his group were travelling. In several places this little stream had lost some of its vitality as soil had eroded away, surrendering trickles of water -- as it always does -- to newly carved-out escape routes in its downhill gravitational flow.

But now, as the riders continued to climb, it became more and more stream-like, with deep cuts in the trail, exposing gravel and larger pebbles, and causing the horses to pick their way carefully between leg-breaking ruts. The ponies, on occasion, dropped their heads to the stream-beds to suck upthe cold liquid nourishment before complying with the prodding encouragement from their riders.

After a mile and a half or so, sloshing through ankle deep water, Jacks guided his grey pony west, off the roadway and up a boulder-strewn drywash.

He looked back, and called out, "We'll head up for a bit, choose a couple of good vantage points and wait for Mr. Jeb Witherspoon and whoever he brings along. We'll have at least one more Ranger before nighttime."

Twenty minutes later they passed beyond a rock formation that satisfied Jacks. He dismounted. From here he had a view of anything that moved below, and the further advantage of the late afternoon sun when that time came. The men and especially, the horses needed rest; the ladies could be untied; and, warned of severe consequences for screaming, even have their gags removed.

The men gathered round Jacks. Crazy Red acted as spokesman for the bunch --

"We'd like to have the ladies, just for a little while... won't do them any damage," the young redhead pleaded. "Been a long time for any of us to have female company, and fer Boo, here, never!"

But Jacks would have none of it!

"Business first! Fun later. Buddy! Take the first watch! Anything move down there just give a low whistle! No shootin' or callin' out, ya hear? You others, get some rest!"

~~~~~
~~~~~

Jacks' dream
Friday Late Morning
June 26, 1840

Pangs of remorse furrowed Jacks' forehead and the regret spread across his face. Why had he let himself bring these ladies along? His quarry was anyone wearing a badge -- namely Texas Rangers -- not a couple of proper ladies. Still in all, one of them was wife to Witherspoon ... and that gave him some sense of demented satisfaction; he'd have her first, before turning her over to any of the others. And having the subject settled, he leaned against a granite spire that towered over his head, confident that his cousin, Buddy, would follow his instructions when their pursuer(s) approached. He began to dream.

Same dream. This time he was even younger. House was on fire. Demons were whooping and hollering on horses outside. His pa went down in a hail of bullets -- his ma was dragged out of the burning house by a lawman -- a badge on his chest. He ran from the flames toward the shed. Another rider wearing a badge tried to swoop down and pick him up, but he was too fast. Shed got set on fire. He crawled on hands and knees to the creek behind the shed. Stayed there, rocking back and forth, his arms around his knees, eyes shut tight. His cousin, Buddy's pa found him two days later -- still in shock, screaming, wandering around in what was left of their blackened cabin. Uncle found his Pa's mutilated body and buried him. Kept calling for his Ma, but never found her. Picked up a six-sided star on the ground next to the remains of the homestead --

stamped on it were some words. Buddy's pa said it said Marshal or Texas Justice or something like that. He swore he'd kill any lawman on sight!

Jacks awoke to the sound of a low whistle. He was still rocking back and forth, sweating -- eyes tightly clamped together, arms around his knees, heart filled with hate.

Chapter 8

Indian Territory
Friday Mid-Morning
June 26, 1840

"Hell, they could have taken any of these ravines, and high-tailed it up into these hills," the blacksmith mumbled, as their horses sloshed on up the road, which by now had become an ankle-deep stream.

"Could have, but didn't!" shot back Drummer. "You see where these rocks have been disturbed? Turned over by hooves. No sir, Kurt! They're still on the road."

Kurt leaned down to see the difference between stone and stone, and had to agree, some were slightly brighter than others; and then with some satisfaction, noted, too, that some of the ruts showed sharper cuts in their sandy walls than one would expect from erosion caused by constant water flow. He concluded, rightly, that they were caused by horses' hooves. This kid knew how to track. Admiringly, the smithy followed the young Ranger's lead.

They'd gone only a couple miles further when Drummer back-tracked a few feet, looked west, up an embankment, then down the eastern slope; retraced his steps back down the road another five or six feet, and chose a rock-strewn ravine heading up the side of the hill.

"This is where they left the road, boys," he announced. "I suggest we go easy. Look at the shale; all those boulders above!"

Squire took over at that point. "Okay, gents, I thought we'd see something like this. It's ambush time. We can't just ride in shooting. That's out. Way too dangerous. Neither can we ride up that slope in a bunch. All it would take is to pry loose a boulder or two to cause a rockslide with all that shale. I have a couple of ideas... any thoughts?"

None came. Squire continued, "I suggest we split up in three pairs: two on the left flank, two on the right, with Witherspoon and another coming right up the center so they see him coming. They have Lottie, so they'll be watching for him. Maybe they'll think he's damn fool enough to ride up here alone."

"An' I wudda!" snarled Witherspoon, glaring at nothing in particular. "Ok, how about this? How about we all go up, as you say, but on foot. Two on the left, two on the right, me in the center, walking my horse, like I was trackin' or sumthin' and Wilson or Kurt handle the other five horses below, an' wave'em up, mebbe in hundred yard stages, on a signal -- like, 'ok, bring'em up' -- as we go. I'll keep lookin' left, then right like I would anyway to avoid bein' ambushed. That way we'd keep eyes on each other at all times."

"Damn fool idea, Jeb!" chortled Harlan. "They could be over that hill and gone halfway to west Texas by now... an' we gonna walk halfway to Lubbock, climb our blistered feet and sorry asses back in the saddle, shake our heads an' say, 'Damn! Looks like we missed 'em'?"

"Now hold on, Franklin! That's probably the best way to get the job done. These Jacks' boys ain't goin' much further. I think, for some reason they're gunnin' for the Texas Militia. A lot of anger went into the hangin' of our three boys back yonder. Jacks must have some kind of vendetta!"

"Yeah, or he's collectin' badges," piped up Wilson.

"I think they're sitting there, waiting for us!" continued Squire. "We all stay behind those rocks as we work our way up that hill, keeping Jeb in our sights at all times."

Turning to his friend, Squire said, "Jeb, you're going to have a target on your chest. Stay close to boulders for your own safety."

Turning to Wilson, Squire nodded, "You just may be right! Maybe he has some damn fool lunatic notion in his head."

And then to them all, "This hill isn't all that steep, nor is it too far to the top. Lottie and Suzanna are waiting up there for us, gents. Stay abreast of one another as we make our way up. Drummer, you're with Harlan up the right flank; Wilson, you come along with me up the left; Kurt, I'll keep you in sight and signal for you to bring the horses up from time to time."

Jeb watched his friends move to left and right of him, and aside from Squire's long glass, each carried only a rifle. They widened the distance to a couple hundred yards on either side. At a signal that they were in position, he pulled his model 1803 Harper's Ferry rifle from its scabbard, readied it, and started up the dry creek bed, slipping on the greasy shale as he went. His big white mare, much more sure-footed, sometimes pulled him along as he hung on to her reins.

And so -- at times cursing Jacks; at times mumbling to his sure-footed white steed; at times, praying for the safety and rescue of Suzanna Knight and his Lottie; at times, thanking The Lord for his five comrades -- Jeb Witherspoon proceeded up the hill.

Chapter 9

Indian Territory
Friday Late Morning
June 26, 1840

Crazy Red stood at Jacks' shoulder, bedecked in the surveyor's grey shroud and peculiar top hat, peering down the ravine at the ant-like lone figure -- a man leading a white horse by the reins, carefully picking his way up.

Jacks shook his head! "Damn fool! What's he expect to do? Climb up here, line us up and shoot us all like so many targets? You gotta hand it to him, though. Takes guts."

Crazy Red Remembers as well
 June 26, 1840

Crazy Red was doing some thinking, too. This indeed is one crazy bastard coming up that hill.

Memories flooded his brain. He smiled. Thoughts of the Kiowa came to mind.

Crazy Red -- at one time known by his Christian name: Bradford Wyman -- the third in a family of five children, born to Terrance and Betsy Wyman in the southwestern part of Kansas. The eldest, Ruby, at fourteen ran off with some cowhand before the family moved to Texas, and was never heard from again.

Terrance Wyman, a proponent of Henry Ward Beecher, was a Puritan "hellfire and damnation" preacher, without the "pure." He laid the law down to all his children with his personal version of the Ten Commandments and a buggy whip.

Betsy, Terrance's wife, had nine children - three of them stillborn. Between pregnancies and live births she had been a schoolmarm. The hard prairie life and harder husband had turned her youthful warmth and caring spirit to bitterness and volatility.

Young Bradford couldn't ever remember a day without a whipping; his back was criss-crossed with permanent welts from a riding quirt. He ran away four or five times -- each time he was returned by townsfolk or neighbors from wherever he had tried to hide, each time his father beat him more severely; each time his mother threatened in that piercing scream to sell him as a slave to the Comanche, which was "a fate worse than death". This continued until one day the Kiowa came, and changed his life forever.

That was the very same day Bradford was determined to rid himself of both father and mother and the other family members once and for all. He'd been given his customary beating, given instructions to chop, split and bring in at least three armsful of wood before supper. He sat, throwing rocks in the pond near the stack of logs, planning his deed in detail: he would use the ax - first on his stronger father, then on his mother. Then he would grab the rifle from over the fireplace and shoot his older, feeble brother. He hadn't worked out his two little brothers, yet, when he noticed the seven shadowy figures approach the cabin.

He watched, transfixed as his older brother, Lucas, was dragged outside, followed closely by his father and mother -- both shouting scriptures mixed with obscenities. He watched as the cabin was set afire, the braves not knowing that there were two yet inside.

And then, the Kiowa discovered him -- red-headed Brandon, laughing madly at the sight before him. One brave yanked the ax away from the youngster, at the same time readying a stone ax of his own to crush Brandon's head, when he was stopped by the obvious leader. His captor brought him forward. The leader, named Teh-too-tsa, as Brandon recalled, took the boy's long red hair in his hand, and muttered something to the others. They all laughed, so Brandon laughed as well.

By this time Brandon's father was screaming obscenities and calling down the wrath of God. One of the braves, at a motion from Teh-too-tsa, pierced his chest with a thrown lance, to the delight, cheering and clapping of the youngster. The chief and those around gazed in bewilderment at the lad's response. Next came the order to, one by one, destroy in heinous fashion, the remainder of the family. Each time, the Kiowa watched for sadness; each time they raised their eyebrows at the smugness, satisfaction and genuine delight at the brutal demise of Brandon's family. He was even invited to scalp his own father, which he did with giddy delight and satisfaction, under the narrowed, stern, disbelieving eyes of the Kiowa troop.

Teh-too-tsa, before the house was set ablaze, had confiscated food and firearms. Now he took the only other valuables the farm yielded: three cows, two horses and Brandon. The lad was tied to one of the horses. The homestead was gone, five lives snuffed out, but this red-headed youngster of perhaps thirteen remained gleeful -- Teh-too-tsa thought him to be special. He turned to his braves and said in guttural, broken Spanish: "Look! We have good medicine! This red-headed crazy medicine man." (*Rojo encabezados por el hombre medicina loca!*) Laughingly they rode away.

Brandon would be with Teh-too-tsa's warriors for eight years, learning to think and act as they did. All was well, until he raped one of Teh-too-tsa's favorite nieces, Princess Laughing Brook, slit the throat and hung the scalp of her brother and future chief, White Wolf, on his belt, then fled on Teh-too-tsa's favorite stallion -- all because he was mocked by her for losing in a tomahawk throw. That was just over half a year ago. Now he was a wanted man -- by Texians and Kiowas alike.

He stumbled onto Jacks and his crew a month or so later, sitting around an evening campfire along the Cimarron River, right in the heart of Comanche Territory, bold as brass, roasting a wild turkey! After a bit of sizing each other up, during which Brandon explained the foolishness of an evening fire in Indian Territory, and the importance of keeping one's scalp, Jacks invited him to throw in with them, And, having no other particular place to get to, he decided there was a bit of strength in numbers, so he did.

~~~~~~~~~

"Well, looky here!" he smiled broadly at Jacks, gripping his shoulder. "Here comes one of them now! Crazy bastard indeed! Let's have some fun, Jacks! Let's drop a boulder on 'im. Might just cause a slide. Maybe pin him to the rocks or give him a ride on down the shale."

"No. -- No, too easy to figure where we are if we try, and fail. I'd rather see his eyeballs in my sights and pull his badge off his chest once he's finished. That way I won't have to go through tons of bloody rocks to find it. We just wait. He'll be here soon enough."

Crazy Red frowned, cursed, kicked a pebble and walked back up the hill where the others sat, waiting.

"Bind the women back up," he ordered. "Put gags back on 'em, too. Boo, grab all the reins. Keep the horses' heads down. No need for a whinny to give our position away. Jacks wants to see that fella's eyes? Let's have him walk right into camp!"

Satisfied that his orders were being followed, Crazy Red once again started back down to where Jacks was kneeling, watching the shale canyon below.
~~~~~~~~~

"Ain't nothin' movin' down there," whispered Jacks. "You s'poze he saw us? I don't see how. Maybe he's ..."

"Mebbe he's takin' a shit. Or pissin' a'ginst a rock!" broke in Crazy Red. "I doubt he saw us. Boys are pretty well outta sight. Hell, they almost scared me when I rounded a corner up there. You just watch and see. He'll be comin'."

Chapter 10

Squire Daniels picked his way carefully up the left knoll overlooking Witherspoon's gulch, Wilson Tanner at his side when possible, and just behind when not; they tried to keep Jeb within sight at all times; but there were those times when a contrary boulder got in the way.

"He's makin' good time," whispered Wilson. "I just hope this little adventure proves worthwhile. I'd hate to see us get to the top, and find only hoof prints down the other side."

"I know, Son, but it's a risk worth taking. That Jacks' bunch and their horses are tuckered out from what Jeb said. Best to hole up somewhere where they have a good vantage point, set out a lookout, and let the ponies rest. That's what I would do, I reckon."

"But what about the ladies? They could be doin' sumthin' shameful to 'em while we're just takin' our time, marchin' up this hill."

"Son, they could be. But I don't think they feel safe enough, yet. When their horses are rested and they feel no one is following them, that's when the ladies will be in trouble," Squire concluded. "Let's just keep moving up this hill."

Squire knew the psychology of men. He had been born into a family of clear thinkers and problem solvers, and had inherited whatever skill-set necessary to out-think most men, although the family used their intellect in "behind the scenes" endeavors -- and, aside from quite actively and vocally espousing the severing of ties with the British Empire during the Revolution, they lived quietly and humbly. His father, Simon, was called upon, and in fact organized the *Committee of Correspondence* in 1772 in Windham, Connecticut, structuring the committee after that of Samuel Adams in Boston. It was a means of underground communication with other cities as to what Parliament was trying to impose upon the colonies, 'vis-à-vis' the Stamp Act, illegal search and seizure, taxation without representation, and more. Other such committees sprang up in New York, Virginia, and practically every other colony. His mother, too, spent hours at Simon's side, drafting these letters, making sure they were accurate for content as well as mechanically; making sure, too, that they were formatted as encouraging and didn't step over the boundaries of obvious sedition.

Squire was born, Noah Ethan Allen Daniels, a moniker he disliked, but of course couldn't change. Born in Connecticut along with younger sister Martha, to Simon and Sarah Daniels, the family of four moved with two other families to central Ohio in 1809 to farm the land. Noah was ten years of age.

When a neighbor decided the land was far too clay-filled to farm, he built a brickworks, and hired the youngster at a quarter a day to haul clay and keep the kiln stoked. Young Noah learned, at his tender age, the value of hard work. He spent half his day farming and half brick-making for the neighbor, Marcus Curtiss, before being home-schooled in front of the fireplace by his mother.

When Curtiss went off to fight in the War of 1812, he left young Noah in charge: taking orders, overseeing the making and delivering of bricks and banking the receipts. Upon Curtiss' return, the lad was offered part-ownership in the brickworks for his industry and integrity; but he declined, explaining that he wanted to explore a bit more of the world at this point in his life. He stayed on with Curtiss only one more year.

Before traveling West, Noah was encouraged, and attended The Medical School of Ohio located in Cincinnati. There he acquired instruction he would use to this day. It was a teaching school for mental as well as physical ailments. There, too, he made the discovery that all men were not created equal.

During his two years there -- 1821 and 1822 -- he gained twenty years' worth of mature thinking, or so he said. Classmates came to him with difficult situations for advice and counsel. His instructors began calling him Squire, at first in jest; but his peers picked it up. The name seemed to suit him; the name stuck. Never again was he Noah Daniels.

He saw the value of an early, free education for those children capable and willing --just as a contemporary out of Massachusetts, Horace Mann strongly advocated. But he also saw, as he himself had witnessed, the misuse of a classroom to force a belief upon an innocent. So he championed the beliefs and rights of the individual over the "right by might" teachings of those instructors at the Medical School -- bent on teaching, as gospel, their own pet theories with not enough science to back it up.

His father encouraged him to become a full-fledged doctor, but his mind was set on the untamed West. Besides, he had read of Samuel Thompson working with herbs back in Vermont, healing peoples' ills naturally. That made all kinds of sense. But in New York, Boston and elsewhere, the doctors being licensed were forced to use a pharmaceutical approach to doctoring -- heavy fines were imposed upon unlicensed herbalists -- Even imprisonment!

No, sir! He wouldn't be involved in the infighting which had already begun in the medical field. He knew enough to field-dress or cauterize a wound, apply poultices, give a man a last drink of whiskey or water, or offer up an appeal to the Good Lord for a dead one. No man needed a degree to help another man. And no law should be able to stop him! He always carried a doctoring kit and a jug of rye in his saddlebag for emergencies on the trail. That, and his wits suited him just fine!

He took a look across to the other ridge. Drummer and Harlan Franklin were just about abreast of Jeb; he and Wilson a bit in front. The ravine angled northwest for some quarter mile further, then it disappeared in the rocks above, and from his vantage point, Squire couldn't tell for sure which direction it would proceed. For sure, there was still some higher elevation to this shale bed, but there would soon be an end to it.

He signaled once more for the horses to be brought forward. As he turned back in the saddle, something glistened, then disappeared, a bit left of his position and further ahead. Wilson had seen it, too.

He caught Witherspoon's eye, and pumped his arm up and down a couple of times to caution Jeb. Wilson finally got Harlan's attention, and did the same. The climbing stopped. Nerves tensed. Senses sharpened.

In character, Witherspoon appeared the only seemingly nonchalant one of the five, though inside he felt a sickening, churning anxiety. He bent over, picked his big, white mare's left front leg off the ground and examined for an imaginary pebble lodged in her shoe. Pulling his hunting knife from its sheath he pretended to dig it out. The afternoon sun was beating down, now, anyway. Wiping sweat from his forehead with his bandana, he appreciated the breather.

"Hell," he mumbled softly aloud, "I may as well find a rock, sit a bit and try to relax in the shade while Squire is looking at somethin' with that glass of his."

Was that simply the sun, finding a piece of sparkling quartzite in the rock above? Squire didn't think so. The sun wouldn't shine on something and just as suddenly move on. No, that shiny thing was moving. What was it? He reached for his long glass and scanned the granite outcropping above.

Chapter 11

Palos Duros Canyon
Friday Late Morning
June 26, 1840

Kgyi-yo (Grizzly Bear) was determined. He and *Apiatan* (Wooden Lance) crept on all fours as they neared the top of the granite face. Earlier this morning *Kgyi-yo* and his three companions had scattered a family of Desert Bighorn Sheep, led by a huge ram. They successfully brought down a small ewe with their arrows, but were able only to put two arrows in the ram before he disappeared among the higher boulder outcroppings. The four quickly fashioned a lodge-pole travois to drag their kill back down the western slope to their raiding party's campsite.

Kgyi-yo motioned for his friend, *Apiatan* to stay, but told the two others to head home. It would not be right to leave a wounded ram in the wild; besides, they needed the meat. So they followed the trail of blood. He was weakening, slowing down, now. Soon he would be theirs.

The young warrior felt a slight twinge of remorse for the slaughter of this magnificent creature. It was his arrow that had struck just behind the shoulder; he was sure of it. But, the warriors below did need the meat. They would praise these two for their skill and tenacity. They would be most thankful. And when they returned home from a successful raid against the Texians or Mexicans, there would be much celebration, some of which would involve the sustenance provided by this hunt. Thinking it through, he felt better.

Apiatan, just over the crest of the rock wall, saw the ram first; standing, not ten feet down the eastern slope, panting, with its great head lowered in exhaustion. He motioned to *Kgyi-yo* with his outstretched arm. Then he pulled his bowstring back to put a final arrow in the beast, but *Kgyi-yo* sternly whispered "No!"

Instead, the young Kiowa warrior, *Grizzly Bear,* stood, walked slowly, stoically down the ten foot slope, his blade now out of its sheath, switching from hand to hand. He faced the ram, now barely inches away; he praised the bighorn's courage, comparing it to his own, explaining that there could be only one end to this struggle. The ram lunged at the young warrior gallantly. Deftly, in one upward deadly thrust, *Kgyi-yo* slit the beast's throat.

When it was over, *Apiatan* joined him, sitting on a smooth rock and watching, as the ram, in its death throes, kicked up dust and caused a river of shale and pebbles to flow down the hillside. The task of hauling their prize back to the camp would require another travois. *Apiatan* disappeared over the crest of the hill to fetch their ponies which were tied a short distance away on the other side, while *Kgyi-yo* gutted the great creature. The hide would be a welcome addition to his teepee. Normally he would take the head back to the village, but not today. Today he was part of a raiding party.

He sat and thrilled at the massive curved horns; from tip to tip they were his bow length across, and his hands could not wrap around the horn at its base.

Apiatan appeared at the top of rock, then progressed down, leading the two ponies. That's when one of them whinnied loudly. An answering whinny from far below startled the braves. For a moment, they stood motionless, peering down the valley floor.

Chapter 12

Palos Duros Canyon
Friday Late Morning
June 26, 1840

Squire's glass found what it was looking for: the tiny figure of an Indian, very close to the rim of the rock wall, walking downward toward a , "What the hell?" he whispered to Wilson. "Why, he's walking right up to a bighorn sheep! He's got a knife in his hand. That's what I saw, glittering! Take a look, Wilson! They're left of those two jagged rocks just below the rim."

Wilson eagerly grabbed the brass and leather spyglass, and at Squire's directive, was able, almost immediately to get the sighting Squire described.

"I'll be!" Wilson whispered hoarsely. "He just killed him, I reckon! Slashed him! Dropped like a stone! Wait! Wait, Squire. They's another one. Comanche, I reckon -- or Kiowa, mebbe."

"Now ain't this sumthin? We're in one hellufa fix here, Squire!" Wilson continued in his hoarse whisper, as he handed the spyglass back to his companion. "They're just sittin' on a stone, watchin' the ol' boy bleed out. We move -- they'll spot us for shore. If Jacks' boys are up there between us and the Comanch... hmmph-ummh! It could get real intrestin!" Wilson finished, shaking his head and scratching his scruff of a beard.

Squire was of the same mind. He sat for a moment, pondering. He needed to get word to the others that they had an unexpected complication. After that, what then?

A few ways to deal with it, he thought:
One — Just wait! The Indians may be so intent on the ram they don't see the others;
Two --- Bring up the horses from the rear and charge up the hill in a frontal attack;
Three --- Continue as planned, slowly, cautiously, and hope the Jacks' bunch won't notice the flank riders until any gunplay starts.

First things first, he concluded, giving the hilltop another scan with the spyglass. Only one warrior in view, now, and he was busily gutting the ram.

Squire stood, hidden from the upper slopes but within view of both Witherspoon and the two men across the way. He held the scope to his eye, then pointed high ahead. Then he gestured as if to draw a bowstring back. Finally, he held up two fingers. Both Witherspoon and Drummer saluted in acknowledgement. Ok! That part is done, Squire thought. Now to figure out the next part. He sat back down with Wilson to get the cowboy's opinion. Wilson shrugged, "I say we should wait. No tellin' how many redskins are on t'other side of that hill. I ain't hankerin' to have my scalp hangin' from no lodgepole, Squire. I got "

Then another complication -- A whinny from the rim above, answered by Witherspoon's white mare. Both men cringed, followed by whispered expletives.

Chapter 13

Crazy Red let out a low curse. "Damn him! I'll kill 'im!" he spat, as he and Jacks in desperate exasperation eyed each other. "I told Boo to keep those horses' heads down and quiet!"

With that, he roared back up to where the other four were huddled together, looks of fright on their faces, gesturing at the rocks above. Boo still clung to the reins of their skitterish horses. The two women were as he had last seen them: tied and gagged.

"I told you..!" he started.

"Shhhh!" That was Isaiah Bernard. "Boo *did* keep the horses quiet!" he whispered icily. "That whinny c-c-came from up there!" he continued, pointing at the rock face above. "The old boy down below is just a d-d-decoy. They've circled round us, and gonna come down the hill for us, sure as shit!"

"We saw dust flyin' from the rim a bit ago," Buddy joined in. "At least, Smitty, here, did. Ain't that right, Smitty?"

The eldest of the outlaws only nodded. His mind was in a dither.

How he got himself mixed up in this troupe of misfits was one helluva head-scratcher. And today he was going to die. Another helluva thing! He was doing just fine in Dodge City.

"Weren't you, Mr. Chester Smitts?" he moaned, aloud.

Uhhh, but for that one poker game -- he continued in his mental stupor -- oh, yeah, and that lady, what was her name? Oh, yeah, LuLu....ok ok, and the whiskey. You had way too much whiskey that night, Smitty ...what was it? Two years ago? Yeah, two years, next month. How time does fly. Here I am, fifty-six years old, actin' like a snot-nosed kid! Shudda found me a good woman and settled down. Maybe one like these two (looking over, and smiling broadly at the two bound and gagged, frightened ladies sitting within eight feet of him) ....ok ok, he thought, ruefully. Not a chance! But maybe a dance hall girl like LuLu....

"I said, *where, exactly*?" An angry voice came to him.

Still sitting, and idly dreaming, Smitty was roused from his stupor by a swift kick on the underside of his boot. Crazy Red's face was six inches from his own.

"The dust! Can you pinpoint exactly where it was?"

"Sure. See them two craggy rocks up yonder?

That's where. An' the whinny came from there, too, I reckon. And the Redskins, too, I reckon."

Ears perked up; all eyes, including the two bound ones, were focused on the old sinner.

"What did you just say, Smitty? Did I hear you right?" Crazy Red demanded in a whisper -- barely audible

"'Fraid so," Smitty croaked. "I thought I saw sumthin' movin' just 'fore I saw the dust, but I tried to pay it no mind. But I've been watchin' that spot since then, and when the horses showed up I was able to make out they had no saddles, an' the "

"Never mind! I see them! There's at least two, and they're looking this way. Must be that Ranger's horse that answered theirs!"

Red continued, "Buddy, keep a rock between you and them and go tell Jacks to get up here! And keep outta sight!"

Chapter 14

It seemed now, Lottie thought, as though Crazy Red, not Jacks was giving the orders. Both men were obviously hot-headed; that much she could see. But now that Indians were involved she feared even more for her life and that of Suzanna's. These killers may be cowards enough to make a dash for the hills, leaving the ladies at the mercy of savages. And she had heard stories of cruel treatment given to all white folk, especially the women.

She had heard that Jeb was below; had to be him, tracking the gang -- and a white horse? Yes, it had to be her Jeb. But Jeb was no match for a party of Comanche. One or two -- maybe even three, sure, but Indians weren't loners, not like, say, a trapper or miner as one might run into out here. No, they ventured from their villages in a party or band of maybe four, six or eight.

Where was Squire? Or the others? There had to be ten to fifteen Rangers across the street while the killing was going on. Some of them she knew. They must be here somewhere, she told herself. They wouldn't leave her husband to rescue her alone. And Suzanna?

Oh, poor Suzanna! Lottie had heard the talk among these men about her father lying dead outside the kitchen door; she had heard Crazy Red bragging about the cruelty inflicted upon all those back at the hotel. What a horrible way to die, she thought. Looking across at young Suzanna, she saw only the horror in the girl's face. I probably look as shocked and drained, myself, she glumly concluded.

"Please, please dear Lord," she began in silent prayer, "though a thousand should fall on my left and ten thousand on my right, please give Suzanna and me the wings of a dove to escape these despicable men."

Dust billowed from the ridge-top above, causing all below to stare. Squire had the best view with his long glass, but the outlaws being much closer were able to make out the cause: one of the horses was dragging a makeshift sled of some kind, with a heavy load on it. In moments it was gone -- over the rim and out of sight, but for the continuing dust. One of the redskins stood at the very top looking down in the direction of his distant audience. He raised his bow and thrust it high over his head in a gesture of strength and defiance, let out a blood-curdling howl that echoed as it caromed against the granite walls. Then he turned to walk up the few feet to the ridge-top.

To the amazement of everyone below, an answering scream and a torrent of obvious verbal contempt and sneering provocation rang out in the Kiowa tongue, just four or five hundred yards above the Rangers' positions, bringing the loin clothed warrior above to stop, turn for a moment, yell something, laugh a long, loud laugh, then proceed to the top and disappear.

"Think he's gone fer good?" Wilson looked pale and anxious.

"No I don't, Son. Not now. Witherspoon will know what he said. I don't speak Comanche or Kiowa, or whatever they said, but my guess is, they were challenging each other. I think it best to put an end to this set-to with Jacks right here and now. No telling what lies on the other side of that ridge, and no telling what that damn fool has done with his braggadocio."

Chapter 15

Jacks was furious as he came up the hill from his lookout position on Witherspoon. "What in hell was that for Red? You gave away our position; there's no way in hell we can surprise that Ranger, we may have Comanche down our throats before an hour's past! And your brain is somewhere up your ass with a fool stunt like that!"

"Ah, come on, Jacks, I just felt like having a bit of fun. He's jus' standin' up there like some great warrior, tellin' the world how great he is."

"And you said?"

Turning to the other men, Jacks said, "Get the women on the horses! Now!"

Turning back to Crazy Red, Jacks demanded, "So, what did you say to him?"

"I said, 'Come down. Only me an' my squaw down here. After she kills you, I will cut out your heart and she and I will feast on it!'"

"An' what did he say back to you?"

"Oh, you know, just some typical horseshit!" Red responded, contemptuously.

"Uh-huh!" Jacks snarled back, narrowing his eyes. And then to everyone, "Mount up! We're goin' over the top! Red, you pull another stunt like that an' I'll put a bullet 'tween your eyes!"

"Uh huh!" Crazy Red sarcastically responded through clenched teeth, staring full hard at Jacks.

Buddy couldn't believe what he was hearing. "Hell, Maywell, this ain't no time to have a pissin' match between you and that crazy som'bitch. That don't make no sense a'tall! They's only one feller down yonder, an' he's wearin' a Ranger badge, sure as shootin'. An', sure, he knows our position now, so ambushin' him is out. But I say we ride down there with our guns drawn an' shoot the shit outta him. We go over that hill, well, the whole Comanch nation could be, mebbe, sittin' an' waitin' fer Crazy Red, here, an' his 'squaw'."

"Kiowa!" laughed Red, scornfully. "He was Kiowa!"

"OK, Kiowa," Buddy growled

The others were nodding their heads at Buddy's logic. Jacks thought about it some more. Perhaps they were right. He looked over at the two women, still bound and gagged, tied to their horse's pommels, then at the other riders, then at Crazy Red.

"You're right, Buddy. I was too hasty. We'll ride right down that fella's throat! I believe that's Jeb Witherspoon down there. Should be a pretty sight for this little filly," he said, pointing at Lottie, "and then," he smiled, "we'll relax the rest of the day!"

"What about the K-K-Kiowa?" Isaiah asked.

"Oh, they should have their hands full. Crazy
Red is takin' his squaw over the ridge to challenge
that young Buck, just like he said. Ain't that right,
Red?" He looked over at Suzanna and smiled. Her
eyes were wide with horror; then began filling with
tears.

"You're the boss, Jacks," the young redhead
answered, smiling. He arranged his grey surveyor's
coat, then pulled his top hat over his ears, his long
greasy, red hair spilling out beneath.

"Come along, darlin'," he quipped, tipping the
top hat, and grabbing the reins of Suzanna's pony.
He pulled the two ponies together, looked Suzanna
in the eyes, smiled, held his finger to his lips in a
"Quiet!" command, and slowly removed the gag from
her mouth. Her first instinct was to scream, but she
held it in; shaking with fright, she slammed her eyes
shut and simply slumped back in the saddle. They
began their long climb, walking their horses slowly
up the shale. Suzanna opened her eyes at last.

"Keep your head!" she whispered to herself.
"Keep your eyes open, your ears tuned! Escape could
be possible." She studied her surroundings -- there
were two spires above her and just to her right. She
could use those as landmarks. And there was a twin
jagged rock formation off to her left. She turned to
view the topography below her, where Witherspoon
was making his way up. There, too, was a landmark:
a distinctive-looking spire, almost looked like a
castle she had seen in a magazine someone had left
at the hotel two years ago. "One thing for sure!" she
spat out, quite audibly, "I will escape or die trying!"

Crazy Red turned in his saddle, "Did you ask
me somethin', Sweetheart?"

Suzanna daggered him with her steely eyes.
"Hee hee hee! Guess it was jus' the wind," he guffawed. *Oh! She is a wildcat!* he thought, smiling.

Chapter 16

Witherspoon grabbed the big white mare's bit with one hand, halter in the other, and looked her in the eye. "Cain't you keep yore mouth shut, just once?" he whispered. "How'my gonna explain this to Squire an' the others?" He shook his head in mock anger, then explained to his four-legged companion that they were supposed to be on an inconspicuous mission. Then he reconsidered, looked her in the eye again, and confessed that he was the one at fault. "Hell, Ol' Girl, I shudda kept yore reins down."

He looked at her again, apologetically, but she just laid her ears back and snorted. Acts almost human, he thought; then smiled. Acts almost like Lottie. The thought brought him abruptly back in focus.

"Cain't just sit here much longer, Squire," he breathed aloud. "Gotta get my Lottie back. Time is a'wastin'."

Jeb poked his nose around the boulder that blocked the view from above, just in time to see the last traces of dust on that western ridgeline --

smoky brown at first, then break up and dissipate into the blue of the afternoon sky. He gauged it was well after midday, some shadows were already beginning to lengthen from the base of the nearby boulder.

A distant, piercing shout made his eyebrows pinch together in sudden concentration. "What the hell?" Witherspoon muttered. He leaned forward, cocking his head, trying to discern the muffled words. "Kiowa, for shore!" He whispered the news to his mare. "Something about great warrior or some such! Too much damn echo!"

That burst of bravado had no sooner traveled to his ears, but a second volley in the Kiowa tongue was hurled right back at the lone warrior on the mountain top, this one coming from much closer -- the outlaw band of "no-goods" no doubt. This time Jeb caught it all.

From close by:
"Come down. Only me an' my squaw down here. After she kills you, I will cut out your heart and she and I will feast on it!"

From the rimrock:
"....Ha! Hide behind squaw! Have no penis! Ha, Ha, Ha!"

Jeb listened intently for more exchange, but none came. "So," he pursed his lips and blew out a sound like a cross between the howling wind and a low whistle; then whispered again to his mare, "We have a Kiowa among that band of 'no-goods'! That explains the savagery back at the hotel. Ain't no sense in holding position, now, Ol' Girl, may as well continue our march up the slope."

He stepped out from behind the boulder leading the big white, and began again to inch his way up the shale-filled gorge. The mare seemed content to stay by his side, though, from time to time she snatched at a rare clump of grass. He looked across at Squire, who nodded his approval, and as he continued on, he saw that Drummer was also on the move, far to his right.

Squire summoned the blacksmith, Farber, to bring their horses on up. Then he pulled his Patterson Colt from its holster, checking it carefully. Wilson watched, intrigued by this new- fangled weapon, then did the same with his flintlock. He also carried a Kentucky rifle which had been handed down from his father.

Both Witherspoon, and Squire on his left, looked up the slope about the same time to see two riders from the outlaws' position slowly meander out from an outcropping of rock some four to five hundred yards away. Up a steep section of ravine they climbed; one rider held the reins of the other horse, whose rider seemed to be tied in the saddle. Squire produced his long glass, to discover a red-headed man wearing some duded out garb, pulling at the reins of a frisky bay mare, whose unwilling rider was none other than Suzanna Knight!

Witherspoon couldn't help himself. He yelled, "Hey you! Bring that girl back here, you coward!" The redhead turned in the saddle, waved briefly, then turned back and continued up at the same pace. Suzanna turned as well, but the only thing that left her lips was a horrific moan of fright.

Squire knew this was the time for action. He turned to see where the horses were. Still some eighty to one hundred yards away at best. He turned again to the sound of other hooves on rock. Horses from above -- seven or eight, all with riders, were bearing down on Witherspoon. One of them, smack in the middle of this small herd and tied to the saddle, was Lottie Witherspoon!

Chapter 17

Birdwell Homestead
Wells, Texas
Saturday Late Morning
June 27, 1840

George Birdwell sat up stiffly in his chair. He pounded on the oak arm with his fist.

"I'll be damned!" he exploded.

"What's got into you, George?" Mona asked, with that look of dread or consternation that always came when her husband suddenly remembered some important clue to a puzzle he'd been whittling on in his brain.

"I need to round up some boys and head back to Brisbie!" He said, getting to his feet. "Jacks! Of course! This is the murderer that I told you about a year ago, Mona."

"You've told me so many things, George. I can't remember them all. I do know you scare me half to death when you jump up and down like that, without warning. Now look what you made me do! I've dropped a stitch. Never mind; I can fix it. Why do you have to go, George? I thought you had a talented Ranger detachment up that way, and just brought in another recruit. What's the matter with them?"

"He's been killing lawmen from Kansas to New Mexico. For some reason it's in his blood. Whenever he sees a badge pinned on someone's chest, he goes after him. He's been credited with ten that I know of. I got wind last year that he's in the Republic. I want to be there when he gets his!"

"If you think you must! I think you give far too much to the Texas Rangers." Mona sighed a long sigh, and continued, "We hardly recognize you when you come through the door anymore. But I suppose I should be grateful," she smiled, wistfully. "You still do walk through that door ever so often."

George wrapped his arms around her in a bear hug, kissed the top of her graying head, then stooped down and cupped her face in his hand.

"Mona, I *always* come home." He leaned in to her, to kiss her again, tenderly. But she met his lips eagerly. They clung together for it seemed minutes, entwined in an exquisitely passionate embrace, before she released him. Then she quickly turned her back so he wouldn't see the worry and tears begin to fill her eyes.

"There's still a couple pieces of chicken from lunch I'll wrap up for you, and I'll fill your canteen," she managed, as George, still fastened to the floor, stood, bewildered. He could never understand women, he thought, least of all, his Mona.

Chapter 18

Palos Duros Canyon
Friday Late Morning
June 26, 1840

The sound of galloping horses' hooves caused both Crazy Red and Suzanna to once again turn to view the rocky trail from which they had just ascended. Ha! Jacks was really going to do it! Red thought. He turned to his very reluctant partner.

"He's running right straight into an ambush, little lady. I can almost guarantee it. That Ol' boy comin' up the valley floor ain't alone. You can bet your -- " then he corrected himself -- "*our* firstborn child!" Red gave a whoop of delight that he had been so menacingly clever with his words.

Suzanna felt repulsed by him. How could anyone, even a man like Jacks, turn her over to this greasy, foul smelling fool? She was certain this madman holding her captive had killed her father; now he's talking of fathering her child? *That will never happen,* she told herself! She would almost rather be back there, hanging from that limb with those three Rangers.

"Oh!" she moaned aloud, then feeling Red's eyes upon her, she caught herself. Mustn't show such weakness, she thought! I shall remain strong in the presence of this beast! Riding past those poor, dead Rangers, though   that seemed ages ago, yet it was a mere few hours -- maybe four or five at most.

"We're just going to sit here a minute," Crazy Red was saying, bringing her thoughts back to the present, "I want to see who lives and who dies."

Waiting didn't take long. An initial barrage of gunfire came from the Jacks' bunch; then came deliberate, single *pops* and *thumps* from the hills on either side of the parched, shallow arroyo.   It seemed the boulders took the brunt of gunplay, as Suzanna heard the *zing* of the lead as it crackled and ricocheted off the stone walls. A few bullets did, however, find their mark.

"Didn't I tell you, sweetheart? Didn't I?" Crazy Red was almost in tears, laughing so hard. "Had to be five or six Rangers in those rocks above. Jacks was smart, though, having that wife of that Ranger, what was his name? Worthington, Willington, Whittingham, whatever; anyway having his wife riding right in the middle. That was my idea you know. Indian tactic, an' a good one."

"Looks like a couple of horses down, and Willington, too, I should think. Hell, they was straight after him. Looks like one of the boys is down, too. Mebbe Buddy or Isaiah. Oh! An' another'n, too. But it shore ain't Jacks. I saw his grey way the hell down the trail. An' I think he's still got a hold of the Missus. Huh! If that don't beat all! Coupla others too, looks like. Kind of a mix-up down the road a piece, cuz there's a few horses comin' up the path, too. Huh! Ranger horses I reckon."

"Well, let's keep going, my dear," Red laughed. "Can't keep our Kiowa friend waiting."

Chapter 19

Palos Duros Canyon
Kiowa Camp
Friday Late Morning
June 26, 1840

Kgyi-yo and *Apiatan* were met with heros' welcomes, as were the other pair of hunters who had preceded them into camp. *Apiatan* told how the ram was a formidable foe, but succumbed to *Kgyi-yo's* prowess.

Once the formalities were over, the young warrior, Grizzly Bear, hushed his companions with the good news: on one of ravines on the eastern slope of the mountain was a band of Whites, perhaps settlers, who were treading on their ground -- taking land given to them by The Great One.

"We will not have to travel many miles on this raid," *Kgyi-yo* smiled. "Our enemy comes to us!" All around him came laughter, mixed with whoops or grunts of approval.

"One speaks the Kiowa tongue," he continued. "Smooth, like honey! But he is coiled rattlesnake! That one is mine!"

"You, my young brother," he turned to a young brave of perhaps fourteen, "will stay with the camp and our supplies. Skin out the ram to dry in the sun. I will write on it when I get back of the struggle and bravery of the ram. It will keep my teepee warm and safe, and I will have the memory fresh every morning when I throw back the hide to enter or leave. If I am not back in three suns, you write on it the story of my bravery, and that I have entrusted it to you for safekeeping!" The youth, Red Hawk, showed at first the disappointment of any deprived youngster, but brightened at the prospect of skinning out the ram, and protecting their camp by himself. He had taken part in several buffalo hunts, and taken part in skinning those huge mammals; he knew the technique well. It would be the same with the ram.

They left the young brave two horses -- one, of course was his own pinto, the other was the pack horse they always used to carry their meager supplies -- a big, strong bay.

Red Hawk waved all seven of his brothers off to battle; then picking up his quiver, adjusting it for ease of reaching an arrow, he held his bow in his left hand, and walked around the campsite twice, inspecting the tiny campfire, insuring there was adequate fuel and kindling to carry through to the next day.

Next he looked to the water supply. The others had taken five skins of water, leaving him two -- enough for his horses and himself. There was a small alpine lake, with stream flowing in and out down the mountain on the northwest side, but the way was very steep and treacherous. He would be wise to conserve water in washing the ram's hide. Before the drying process he would use the scraping and rubbing process he had seen the women and elders use on buffalo hides. They usually used sand and special blades just for that purpose, but Red Hawk would improvise; he would use ground shale to clean the hide of any clinging flesh; then almost no water would be necessary.

The other stores, mostly dried pemmican and fish, were adequate. Finally satisfied that he had sized up his personal situation maturely, Red Hawk eagerly set about the task at hand.

He began by carefully cutting around each hoof with his hunting knife. Grizzly Bear had gutted the ram on the mountainside -- had even cut its head off already, leaving those parts for scavengers; so it was a simple matter, now, to start from the legs and cut up to the incisions already made: from the soft, white underside of each front leg to the throat, and from the underside of each hind leg to the tail end of the flapping hide that once held the stomach. He was able to roll the ram from side to side to accomplish that part of the task, but discovered that the rest of the job wasn't quite so easy. The squaws could skin out a buffalo very quickly. Why couldn't he?

He sat for a moment, looking over the gorge that came all the way up to where the raiding party had set up camp. It was as if the mountain had opened its mouth and swallowed everything -- trees, rocks, vegetation, everything! It's so desolate, he thought; desolate, but beautiful.

He could see the trail he and his companions had taken yesterday morning and wondered that they knew the way, so overgrown it was with tall grasses and juniper trees. He could see the ribbon of river meandering in the grassy plains far below to the west. He wasn't really that high up, but he thrilled at the beauty and ruggedness before him! *Apiatan* had told him the name the Mexicans had given this place -- what was it? *Profundo barranco de palos duros*. Yes, that was it! The deep canyon of hard sticks.

Again, Red Hawk concentrated on skinning the ram. He managed to peel the hide from both forelegs all the way to the neck, then made two piercings in the tough neckhide. Next, he ran a strip of rawhide rope through the holes, looped it and tied it off. Then he pulled for all he was worth on the rawhide. The hide wouldn't budge. He needed more strength. Or, he told himself, "I need more patience."

So, it was back to his razor-sharp knife. Slowly, holding the knife at a proper angle, and slicing ever so gently, he managed to separate the hide from the animal's flesh, fractions of an inch at a time, until at last, working alternately from side to side and from both ends, he had only the center of the back left.

Now he gave a giant heave on the rawhide rope. The hide easily pulled free from the ram. He examined his work. Not a hole in it other than the two in the neck which he had made, which he would soon cut off, and the one behind the shoulder from Grizzly Bear's arrow.

Red Hawk laid the Ram's hide inside out with legs outstretched, and pinned them to the earth with sharpened sticks. Next he dragged the Ram's carcass to a flat rock the others had used earlier to cut the ewe up in chunks.

Almost exhausted from the struggle, the young lad thought he heard a noise, like falling rocks on the south slope. He cocked his head to concentrate. Nothing! After twenty to thirty seconds holding his breath, he decided rocks can sometimes slide down hillsides seemingly without an outside cause. Nevertheless, he decided to make another patrol of the perimeter before continuing with the ramhide preparation.

The afternoon sun was still in the sky, but now shadows were playing with the boulders, some of the scrub larchwood and junipers were creating eerie images, causing Red Hawk's spine to tingle. He grabbed an arrow from his quiver and placed the notch onto his bowstring, then began his tour.

There! He heard it again! Closer, coming down a different ravine from the one taken by his party, yet from the same general direction. Red Hawk waited behind a boulder. He saw a horse's ears and head appear between some boulders, then the horse, then a second horse with a white lady tied to it. Finally, he heard a man's voice, speaking a greeting in Kiowa, but certainly not a voice he recognized.

At last, he saw a strange black hat appear into the open. This is the man *Kgyi-yo* had warned about. Red Hawk couldn't take chances. He drew back on his bow. The arrow pierced the redhead just where the left shoulder joined the torso. Crazy

Red's gun discharged harmlessly into the air as the man let out a cry that echoed down the eastern gorge, then the redhead slumped to the ground.

Red Hawk stared at the man's crumpled frame, saw that he was still breathing, though dazed, in shock and near death -- blood beginning to turn the ground red around him. Then he turned his attention to the woman. He tried to pull her down from her horse, but she was securely tied to the saddle. He cut her bonds. At that point, she gave him a swift kick to the side of his face and, urging her horse, scrambled up the same path she had just come down. Red Hawk got to his feet, holding his bruised cheek in time to see her disappear over the rim.

Chapter 20

Palos Duros Canyon
Friday Early Afternoon
June 26, 1840

Witherspoon saw the riders coming at him at a gallop; it almost seemed, in slow motion. He could see his dear sweet Lottie's face in the bunch, riding behind a big grey, ridden by a faceless fellow. Jeb's eyes could only focus on his wife.

As the outlaws neared him, Jeb let loose the white's reins, and sprang behind a small granite spire for cover. Bullets were pinging off the rocks, a horse fell within ten feet of him -- its rider, moaning with pain, crawled to a nearby stone and hid behind it. Return fire was coming from somewhere above, but Jeb couldn't fire a shot. He could only see the fear in Lottie's eyes as she rushed by him, reins pulled along by that lead rider on the grey.

Some of the riders, in a confused state, circled their horses for another run at Witherspoon, but that lead fellow, still hanging on to Lottie's horse continued down the ravine, followed by one other. Then the sound of Drummer's smoothbore brought another rider down. This one didn't move. His mount fell as well, but staggered to its feet, snorted, and trotted up the ravine, hind legs kicking as it went.

Squire thundered from somewhere in the rocks above, "Drop your guns, fellas! Texas Rangers! You're surrounded!"

Most of those below did as instructed, but one of the outlaws, already doubled over in pain from a gunshot, managed to spur his pony down the gorge, avoiding a second bullet that whizzed by his head and careened harmlessly off a boulder.

"Let him go!" Squire shouted. "Somehow, I don't think he'll get too far. He was hurting pretty bad from the look of it."

"Witherspoon! You okay?"

"Just a scratch! I gotta git after Lottie, though, Squire. Don't have no time to have you fuss over me." Witherspoon was collecting weapons from the ground where members of the Jacks' band had tossed them, as the blacksmith, Kurt Farber, came riding up with their horses.

Then, as the other Rangers were climbing down the rocks to join Jeb, they heard Kurt saying, "There's another one, just a kid, down the road a bit. I think he's dead, but I didn't stop to see for sure. He fell off his horse right in front of us -- me and the horses."

"One over there behind that rock, too," said Witherspoon. "He's been awful quiet the last few minutes. That's his horse layin' there, I expect."

Wilson went to where Jeb had pointed. "No, he's still alive. Shot in the laig an', looks like the side of his head, but he's still breathin'."

Squire took a look at the outlaw lying behind the little craggy rock. "Bring me my medical kit, would you Harlan? It's in my bag."

"Drummer, you and Wilson hog-tie those other two," the boss-man instructed. "We'll question them later, but right now I'm kind of busy."

Harlan looked incredulously at the Ranger crouched over the barely breathing miscreant and whistled, "Shhhhhit, Squire!" And then very deliberately, "Why don't you jist shoot that sonofabitch and be done with it!"

"He's no longer a danger, Harlan. Now he's just a cowpoke with a bullet in his leg."

Franklin pulled Squire's kit out of his saddlebag, shaking his head as he came back to his comrade.

"If you save his life, Squire Daniels, and he turns around and shoots you "

Harlan was cut short by a holler from young Drummer: "We got more company comin' down the mountain! Injuns!" he shouted.

"I count seven!" Witherspoon yelled. Then he added, "One helluva day!"

The Rangers scrambled for cover as the Kiowa band descended on them, whooping and screaming. Sounds of rifle and pistol fire filled the air. This is what Grizzly Bear expected. Now his band would have the advantage while the Rangers were reloading.

But Grizzly Bear had not heard of the Colt Patterson #5 revolver. His braves turned to make a closer run at the Rangers, but they were met with unforeseen devastation; at least twenty to twenty-five rounds were fired; four braves fell immediately,

besides two ponies -- Grizzly Bear was perplexed -- and, for the first time in his life, he knew fear!

Kgyi-yo sped up the ravine, his two remaining braves close behind, to regroup and discuss their circumstances. It would be a disgrace to retreat and go home with no trophies, yet wisdom told him to abandon this effort. They were no match for the guns that shoot without reloading.

Chief Teh-too-tsa would understand. They were completely outnumbered. They would mourn the loss of *Apiatan* and the others, and make an oath to take revenge against these white usurpers of their lands and hunting grounds. **Teh-too-tsa** would nod his head sagely, and vow the vow of all Plains Indians: "Even if we must, we shall join the Apache, Comanche, and Arapaho, to destroy our common foe, the white man."

Chapter 21

Palos Duros Canyon
Friday Early Afternoon
June 26, 1840

"Who's ridin' with me?" Witherspoon wanted to know. "Drummer? Wilson? Drummer, I could use your trackin' skills; I know the direction they went, but who knows where they're headed?"

"Sure, Jeb, but first let Squire take a look at that left arm. That ain't no scratch!"

Blood was trailing down the shirt cuff of the older man, and dripping on the stones.

"Keep quiet! I told you, I'm okay!" Witherspoon bellowed. "It's gettin' late!"

Squire had heard the exchange between the two, and promptly hustled over to his old friend.

"A 'through and through'. Lucky it didn't hit bone, old man!" He poured a bit of whiskey on the wound, wrapped it tightly with a torn shirt sleeve, and, turning to Drummer, said, "Just watch him. If he starts shivering, shoot him."

"You can bet on it," smiled Drummer.

"Assholes! Both of you!" snarled the Ranger. Squire watched as the two rode out of sight down the gulch, then back to the task at hand; now, however, there was another wounded one: a Kiowa brave pumping blood from a belly wound -- and even, possibly a third -- that fellow from Jacks' band down yonder that Kurt had mentioned. He instructed Wilson and Kurt to, first of all, tie the Kiowa's hands behind his back, and hobble him. Then he sent Wilson and Harlan down the ravine with an extra horse to pick up the fallen rider.

In the meantime, Squire continued where he had left off: examining the injured Jacks' man. The fellow was just awakening from the bullet scraping the hair off his left temple, or the rock his head was laying on. In either case, he was losing a lot of blood from his two wounds. Squire judged him to be over fifty, and verbalized such to the blacksmith, who concurred.

"Kurt, I have a clean shirt in my saddlebag. Run, grab it for me. I was supposed to get married in it," he said to the big man, eyes twinkling, "but hell, she won't mind a little blood."

"You have a woman, Squire?"

"No. Just a dream. Might become a reality someday." He chuckled to himself. He could just hear one of Witherspoon's favorite sayings: *"Hell, they's always a someday!"*

The others were in sight now, with a body slumped over the saddle. "Didn't make it Squire. It's that kid that came in the *Copperhead* this morning, lookin' for his sister."

"Anything in his trappings?"

"No," came the reply.

"Nothing? Well then, we have some burying to do. Three, maybe four Kiowa, the youngster, and that other Jacks' hombre that Drummer ripped up with that scatter gun of his." Daniels shook his head and continued, "And that's just for starters," he finished, looking disgustedly at the two outlaws they had tied and thrown against a stone. "Just for starters," he repeated. "Not sure we have enough dirt that can be dug into around here," he continued, "but we should try. Deep as you can and throw a few stones over them," was the ruling from Squire.

The Ranger ripped up the shirt into strips, soaked a strip in whiskey, then pushed a stick in the outlaw's mouth while pushing the soaking bit of cloth in the hole in the old man's leg.

A bellow of pain burst from the outlaw's clenched teeth, followed by a few expletives.

"If nothin' else, he's awake," Wilson grinned, as he walked by, looking for a place on this granite mountain with a bit of dirt.

Without hesitation, Squire wrapped the fellow's head in more of the shirt, and poured a bit more whiskey over his left temple. This time the fellow just slammed his eyes shut and bit down hard.

~~~~~~~

"Now for the Kiowa," Squire said aloud to anyone listening. He offered the outlaw a taste of whiskey, readily accepted, before moving on; then
~~~~~~~

he turned back.

"Hey, Harlan!" Squire shouted to the young Ranger. "Got a better idea. Those three Kiowa -- bring them over here by this one," he motioned. "We won't bury them. We'll put them on their horse mats. Grab all their truck -- their bows, knives, water pouches, get it all. Stretch them out, maybe three feet apart, on their backs, facing west."

"Now, what the hell's got into you, Daniels? First you save that bastard that killed our boys! Now you're gonna honor these savages? I'll have no part in it!" Harlan ignored Squire's order, and stormed off to bury the two outlaws. That much he would do.

Wilson, small shovel in hand, looked back at Squire, who was smiling a wry smile. The Double Bar S cowboy had that, "Now what do I do?" look on his face.

Squire motioned for him to come. "Let him bury those two. You gather up those three redskins, and drag them over here, along with their fittings. Franklin obviously belongs down in Trinity country," he laughed, loud enough for the younger Ranger to hear. From beyond his vision Daniels heard the melodic hum from a recognizable tune, and the sound of shovel on stone.

~~~~~~~

"Now for the Kiowa," Squire said a second time, and walked to where the red man lay.

The warrior, a chisel-faced, handsome figure of a man, was leaning almost prone, against a boulder. He was obviously in agony; but he
~~~~~~~

mustered all the bravado he could, and sat proudly. The brave watched Squire approach with a canteen and some strips of cloth. He wouldn't allow this man to touch him! But, in the end, he had no choice; three men gathered round him and held him down and in his exhausted state he was no match for them.

The one called Squire poured water in his wound and bent to examine it. He tried to bite him, but Squire was too fast. Then the white men sat on a couple of stones and stared at him, mumbling among themselves. *Strange*, he thought, *the way they would say "Hmmmm," and rub their necks.*

"He's got a bullet stuck in his right side," Squire reported. "I need to build a little fire and cauterize that wound or he'll bleed to death. If I'm lucky I can remove the bullet while I'm at it."

"I tell you, Squire, this ain't right!" Harlan burst out, just returning from the burial, brow wet with dusty sweat. "By thunder! You go around shootin' these devils be they white or red, then you patch 'em up. You must be practisin' to be a doctor when you retire from the Rangers Damn!"

But, his feelings aside, Harlan piled up some branches of dry brush; then he and Kurt set about to build a little fire. Wilson, meanwhile, dragged the Kiowas over and laid them out on their riding mats as instructed. The Kiowa warrior watched suspiciously through narrowing eyelids.

Now ready, Squire again had the others hold the brave down. He tried to insert a twig between the warrior's teeth but it was rejected each time. He finally told his patient he wouldn't argue. His knife blade almost white hot, went quickly from fire to flesh. The Kiowa jerked upward and, just as quickly, slumped back to the earth.

"Ok, boys, now to get that slug out of him while we still have light to see. Find me a strong stick a foot long or so, and sharpen one end; we'll dig it out."

"What's the matter with one of his own arrows?" Kurt asked.

"Splendid idea! That may be even better! If we can't dig it out, we may be able to push it through, at least enough to grab it out of his side."

And that's what they did.

Squire poured whiskey in both ends of the hole and cauterized both wounds. Next, he wrapped the brave's middle in the rest of the shirt, left one of the Kiowa's water pouches half filled with water, left a bit of buffalo jerky the Indians had brought with them; then as a gesture of good will, Squire left the brave his bow, his quiver with just one arrow, his knife, and another water pouch, this one with just a few swigs' of whiskey left in it -- he put this all within reach.

Turning back to the just-bandaged outlaw, Daniels demanded, "What's your name?"

"Chester Smitts, and before you tell me I made a mistake being here today, rest assured, I made that mistake long before today. I'm supposed to die today. I could feel it. All day long I could feel it."

"My name is Squire Daniels, Texas Ranger. You won't die today if I can help it, Chester, but I'm taking you back to Brisbie, and I think you will die soon for what you and your friends have done to some mighty good folks. Who killed the hotel man and the Indian boy?"

"They was kilt by Crazy Red. That man is plumb nuts! Jacks shot the three Rangers while they was swinging on ropes. Isaiah, that fella over there," he said, pointing in the direction of the two that were hog-tied, "helped him string 'em up. Matt an' me, we kep' sayin', 'Jus' shoot 'im. We ain't got time to hang 'im, if we're gonna get to town tonight', but Jacks, he just kep' sayin' he's makin' a statement to ever lawman walked the earth."

"Uhhuh! And who was leading that lady up the gorge a while back?"

"Thet was Crazy Red again. He an' Jacks had a blow-up. He'll torture her for shore, then prob'ly scalp her. I'm tellin' you, he's crazy as a loon!"

"Uhhuh!"

Squire then ordered Franklin, along with the blacksmith, to round up as many of the horses they could find, especially the saddled ones and the one laden with goods that had been stolen from Brisbie's hotel. Then they unceremoniously hoisted the two hog-tied killers onto two horses, winched them down on the ponies' underbellies, using the stirrups, as chocks to hold the human cargo fast, while the injured Smitts they allowed to ride, sitting in his saddle.

Thus prepared, Harlan Franklin along with Big Kurt Farber began the trek back to Brisbie -- five men, and a string of ponies: two Indian, four saddled -- one with the rescued goods from the *Good Night.*

Wilson, from the Double Bar-S turned to Squire. "You shore got under Harlan's skin there, Squire," he laughed.

"Oh hell, Son. Soon as he's around the next

bend, 'twill all be forgotten," the Ranger replied. "Got to 'vent' sometimes. Good for the soul. Now, let's go find Suzanna, and put an end to this 'Crazy Red'."

So the two continued up the mountain in search of Suzanna Knight and Brandon -- Crazy Red -- Wyman, leaving the three dead warriors, facing the setting sun, lying dead on their horse pads, each with his bow and one symbolic arrow. Lying next to them was the breathing Kiowa, "Wooden Lance" -- *Apiatan* -- still unconscious, leaning against the boulder.

Chapter 22

Palos Duros Canyon
Friday at Dusk
June 26, 1840

Evening was stretching out its long shadowy fingers as Suzanna urged her pony down the western slope of the canyon. She would double back; take another route to get back to the Rangers she had seen, but right now she needed to get away from the proximity of that madman and the Indian encampment. A quick look had told her she was in a dangerous place. Fortunately, it was manned by only one brave, and he, but a youngster.

She had never prayed for a killing before, but now she prayed the boy had incapacitated Crazy Red for good! She prayed the Rangers would kill them all! She prayed for Lottie's safety and for that brave husband of hers walking straight up that ravine in plain sight. Then she prayed for her own safety.

"Dear Lord," Suzanna whispered, "I have read

your word. I have read that Your Rod and Your Staff shall guide and keep me safe, even when I am in a deep valley, surrounded by my enemies. Lord, help me to trust You. I have never been so scared in my life, and truly! I am in a shadowy valley! Amen!"

Then Suzanna thought of the three Rangers, Timmy, and her father, and added a bit more to her prayer: "I pray You will raise them up in the first resurrection to be with You forever. Amen."

She needed to circle around toward the east. That was now a "must" with dusk approaching. She found a very narrow trail -- probably a deer trail she decided. Perhaps that would lead in the right direction. But after some thirty feet, it followed another gorge down the slope, but still traveling westward. She reined her pony in, then swung it back around, to retrace her steps.

She decided she should occupy her mind with something other than the fear she felt, and hit upon just the thing: her pony should have a proper name. She ran several through her mind as they trotted through the underbrush in the waning light: Sage, Beauty, Sugar foot, Sundown; none seemed to fit until she struck upon *Courage.*
"That's it!" she whispered in the little sorrel's ears. "You and me, Courage! We're survivors! Let's find our way back to Brisbie!"

A startled mule deer crossed just in front of her, as Suzanna started back up the way she had come, giving her new hope. Ah, perhaps this big buck was sent just for her guidance! He was on his way for an evening drink from the river below! So he was traveling west, Suzanna concluded -- which meant he was coming, hopefully, from the east!

She searched the area where he had first appeared. There it was! A second path!

At her urging, Courage hopped up a two foot ledge composed of granite, and continued up the winding trail, between Junipers and scrub brush.

Once again Suzanna prayed aloud in a quiet whisper, "Thank You, Lord. Thank you for that deer, for the trail, and for Courage... uh, the horse, I mean." Then smiling, added, "And give me courage to keep strong as Courage and I travel this little trail together!"

The trail wound up and up the rugged ravine, sometimes between a series of rock outcroppings, or an occasional Mesquite or Juniper, sometimes seemed to disappear, but Courage never once hesitated. She moved forward as though she was very well acquainted with every inch of it, and Suzanna simply gave the horse its head. And they were definitely traveling east!

The trail at last came out of the brush on a flat mesa. From here, Suzanna could see north and south and, of course, west. The rim was just ahead of horse and rider, and from there she would be able to catch a glimpse of the eastern slope -- before it was locked in nightfall. With luck, -- "No! With God's guidance!" she told Courage. "And yours! Now, we need to find that trail we came up."

She urged Courage onward. The sorrel, as though she had complete understanding, sprang forward immediately, covering the thirty feet of shale at a fast canter.

They were over the rim and had just begun their search for a downward trail when Courage snorted, and bounced sideways. Suzanna saw at once where they were: the jagged twin peaks she had marked in her mind. But something was wrong.

"What is it, girl?" she asked, and then she saw; two coyotes snarling and tugging at the remains of a dead beast of some kind. When they saw her, they very reluctantly backed off to allow horse and rider to proceed downward in their quest for the trail. As they passed by, Suzanna saw the rack and remains of a head from a large mountain sheep.

"Disrupted your dinner, did we? Go on back. We're not quite in the right spot anyway," she told them. "We need to go more to the left...just north a bit. Then I think Courage and I will find the trail we're looking for."

There was a certain solace talking to the horse and the coyotes. She felt much safer, somehow. They hugged the rim and cut straight across for some three hundred yards, Suzanna holding a steady conversation with the sorrel, until she found that outflow of shale, and gave out a jubilant, "Oh, Thank You, God! Courage, look! We're almost home!"

Courage, sensing something good was happening, broke into a trot as she made her way down the shale. She sometimes slid, momentarily losing her footing, but regained it quickly and continued on. It seemed to Suzanna they covered the distance in less than half the time it took for Crazy Red to drag her up that mountain. She wanted to shout for joy, but thought better of the idea, still not knowing the outcome of today's confrontation.

Daylight had long ago turned to twilight on this, the eastern slope, and by now the young lady was having difficulty seeing. Should she stop here for the night, or continue down the trail? She hesitated for only a moment; she would continue until she was forced by the dark to quit for safety's sake.

"No moon in the sky tonight, Courage, but look at those stars! I suppose we could just follow the Dipper or Orion to get back to Brisbie. What do you think?" she asked her new best friend.

For a moment Courage didn't answer. Then, as earlier, the mare snorted, followed by a cross between a grunt and a scream. Then, as if that wasn't enough of a warning for her rider, she backed up about three feet, all the time grunting and blowing out between her rubbery lips. Then she stood still, quivering.

Suzanna tried to cut through the darkness with her eyes, but could not. Something caused this equine outburst, but what? She dismounted. Holding the reins, she moved cautiously forward. She caught the faint but distinct smell of mesquite, and a few feet more she saw the source: the glowing embers from an almost dead campfire, some twenty feet away. Nothing more. No figures around the fire, no quiet discussions or laughter, no horses -- just the red glow and a wisp of smoke.

Suzanna started to guide the mare forward, but again, Courage jerked her head and snorted.

"Okay, girl," Suzanna whispered. "I'll take a look, and let you know what I find."

Suzanna wrapped Courage's reins around a small Juniper, told her to stay calm and quiet, picked up a good-sized rock, and walked cautiously to the small bed of coals.

"I need more light," she told herself aloud, and searched in the dark for a dead mesquite branch. Finding a suitable one, she poked it in the embers. Within seconds the Mesquite burst into flame. She held the burning bush over her head and in the shadowy dancing light she saw a ghastly scene: four Indians, Comanche or Kiowa, she couldn't tell which, were laid out under a tree, three were lying flat, one was propped up against a boulder. But all were dead.

"No wonder you were skittish, Girl," she called out to Courage. "You could smell death, couldn't you? Good Girl!"

There was an easy supply of mesquite to keep the fire going; Suzanna decided to spend the night. But she would take the coals to a further location, so Courage and she could feel a bit more at ease. She chose a spot on the opposite side of a nearby boulder, and started a second fire. Then she brought Courage to a closer tree and tied her off there.

"Sorry, Girl. I'd take your saddle off, but we might need to move fast in the night." Courage nuzzled her neck in response.

Suzanna curled up by the fire for the night, to the typical night sounds one would expect to hear in the high plains of north Texas in 1840 ....until a sound very unlike the others reached her ears -- the sound of approaching horses.

Chapter 23

Kiowa Camp
Palos Duros Canyon
Friday Evening
June 26, 1840

Evening was coming on, with evening birds in fine form, warbling their favorite songs as *Kgyi-yo* and his two companions appeared in the clearing, and assessed that which lay before them. A totally unexpected situation -- a very much wounded white man with flowing red hair lay in the middle of their trail!

This was the **red-headed crazy medicine man** (*rojo encabezados por el hombre medicina loca!*) **Teh-too-tsa had taken under his wing almost ten years ago -- the one who raped and killed, and fled the Kiowa village just a few moons ago.**

Ahhh! Grizzly Bear determined, this is the one who challenged me a few hours ago in the Kiowa tongue, the one who had said his squaw would kill me and eat my heart while it still beats in my chest! The one who is no match for my young

cousin, Red Hawk's arrow. Where was his squaw, now, to protect him?

Red Hawk came running. "Oh, I am sorry, *Kgyi-yo,*" he blurted out in Kiowa, expressing remorse. "I know you said this one was yours, but he came so fast I had no time to think. I am sure my arrow does not cause death," he added, looking up at his mentor.

Grizzly Bear held up his arm as if to say, "It is no matter", then, puzzled, looked at Red Hawk's cheek. "Did he do this to you?" he asked, pointing at the boy's swollen face.

"No. The crazy one's squaw. She..."

"His *squaw!*" *Kgyi-yo* almost screamed out the word in manic astonishment, his eyes widening. "He brought up his squaw to fight me?" Then, as the others dismounted and moved closer to this verbal exchange between Uncle and nephew, *Kgyi-yo,* regained his composure. "Where is this squaw?" he shouted. "I fear her not!"

A weak male voice came from behind them. "She'll squeeze your life from you with her bare hands!" it cackled, "then hang your scalp from her waistband."

All four warriors wheeled around to see Crazy Red, propped up on his one good elbow, smiling a ghastly smile in the dim light of evening, enhanced by the shadowy dance of Red Hawk's fire.

"If I know her like I think I do, it will happen tonight." Crazy Red continued, "No moon. Good for hunting. You'll all be dead. I may be wrong, but if not tonight, very soon..... hee-hee-hee-hee," Red finished.

"Quiet!" *Kgyi-yo* shouted.

One of his companions rushed to quiet the redhead forever, but was stopped with a word from Grizzly Bear. The Kiowa leader dismounted, and walked stiffly to the white man on the ground, knelt down, and smiled.

"Ah! My friend, *rojo encabezados por el hombre medicina loca!*" Grizzly Bear assured him, "I have no intention of killing you! I shall deliver you to Teh-too-tsa. He shall determine your fate!"

The wounded white man's only reaction was a wistful smile; then, in as loud a whisper as he could muster, "Her name is Blood Woman. She'll be here for you soon." Again he laughed a haunting laugh.

Kgyi-yo stood and turned to go.

"Oh by the way, *Kgyi-yo,* I have no intention of killing you! I have already turned you over to Blood Woman. She shall determine *your* fate!"

Kgyi-yo turned to respond, but found himself staring down the barrel of Crazy Red's pistol, which no one had bothered taking from him.

For the second time Grizzly Bear felt real fear. He gritted his teeth. How much of what was said was overheard? He walked as calmly as he could back to the others.

"Leave the crazy one alone!" is all he said. But he knew: they had heard -- and worse, they had seen.

"The fire is low," Grizzly Bear's voice was strong. "We shall make it blaze!" he instructed. "We shall watch for his squaw, Blood Woman, to return!"

~~~~~~

Flickering shadows of light could be seen dancing on the boulders far up the ravine, possibly even, beyond the rim. The Rangers looked at each other, quizzically.

Wilson spoke up in just barely audible tones, "What the hell you spoze that's all about, Squire?"

"Campfire, I reckon," came the whispered reply. "Mighty big one though. Might be the girl, signaling. But I expect not. She wouldn't have a fire that big unless it got away from her. But that makes no sense either. Not enough fuel for a range fire on top of a pile of boulders. Well, we're heading that way anyway. We'll soon find out."

"How long you bin a Ranger, Squire?" the young cowboy asked quietly. "You think I'd make a good one? I bin thinkin' on it ever since Birdwell swore me in temporary."

"That depends entirely on you, Wilson. I'm happy. It's a free kind of life; being your own boss, basically. You certainly won't get rich, but there are some extras along the way, and you're not tied down to a ranch foreman's rules. We size things up according to our conscience, make judgment calls, and adhere to a strict moral code: fair play for everyone. I don't, for instance, kill an Indian simply because he's an Indian. But if he tries to burn a settler's house down, then it's a whole different story."

Wilson pursued that line. "Well, then, what if that settler shot the redskin first?"
~~~~~~

"As I said, Son, we make a judgment call. Now, shhhhush! That fire is just down this little grade," Squire whispered.

The older Ranger dismounted, and drew his Patterson, the young cowboy followed suit, pulling his flintlock, but Squire motioned for him to holster his weapon, and instead handed Wilson his second colt revolver.

They tied their horses off to some junipers, and crept toward the eerie shadows on the boulder walls. Rounding a bend, they came to the Kiowa camp. A young buck was throwing more mesquite on the flames; sparks flew into the sky all around the warrior, and brilliant light and smoke momentarily caused him to close his eyes and grimace in reaction, turning unseeing, in their direction.

As the Rangers stared, one of their horses providentially snorted. The warrior opened his eyes just long enough to spot the two faces staring at him, and shrieked in the Kiowa tongue, "Blood Woman!" He threw the mesquite sticks in the air, and ran for his horse. In the split seconds that followed, a raspy voice from somewhere to the Rangers' left echoed in Kiowa, "Blood Woman! Ohhhhhheee! Hee-hee-hee-hee!" The other Kiowa chased after the first, and in a matter of seconds all were galloping down the dangerous western slope, leaving behind their supplies, the fresh meat, the ram's hide, everything.

~~~~~~~~~~~

As Wilson searched through the camp and its surroundings, Squire searched the area from where that voice had come, and stumbled across the half-
~~~~~~~~~~~

dead Crazy Red, lying where he had been dropped by the young warrior's arrow.

"Where's the girl?" he asked gruffly.

"Oh, you mean my squaw, Blood Woman?" the redhead smiled weakly. "I don't really know. Chasing those Kiowa down the mountain I expect. Hee Hee! Did you see them? Scared as all get out!"

Squire seized the weapon from the redhead's fist, then half-carried, half-dragged the scoundrel next to the fire by the one good arm, ignoring the cursing and crying out by the outlaw.

"I couldn't use my gun if I wanted to, Ranger. It ain't even loaded," the redhead sobbed, between convulsive, painful gasps. Then the pain was too much. The wounded man fell unconscious.

"Nothing here but a coupla water pouches an' a staked out sheep hide!" sang out Wilson. "Looks like a lot of meat, though! I don't think we should stick around here, Squire. They'll be back fer shore when they git over their jitters."

"I tend to agree," Squire shouted. Then, "Well, I'll be! Hey, Wilson!" He continued, "This fellow's packing a pretty full money belt! Might be ..." Turning, he found his companion had come back to the fire and stood close by, so he continued in a normal voice, "might be one of those extras I was telling you about, but we won't know that until we're back in Brisbie. Now I need to put a plug in him, then we'll go back down to where the other Kiowa are, and spend the night."

"What about the meat?" Wilson wanted to know.

"If his saddle pony is anywhere near, we'll take it. Otherwise we leave it. We'll be packing this fellow down."

"Ain't no pony, but I think I'll cut off a slab, just so's in case we end up hungry, at least we got sumthin' to chaw on."

"Alright, but use something to wrap it in. Now, bring me a fire brand from the fire. I'm going to need your help." The young man eagerly complied. "Okay," Squire continued, "when I jerk the arrow out, you shove that stick in the hole for a couple of seconds. Ready?"

~~~~~~~~

When it was over, Squire pitched the unconscious outlaw over the saddle, and climbed up behind. He smiled as another of Witherspoon's favorite sayings came to mind: *"This has been one helluva day!"*

Wilson shook his head, "Is this one of those 'judgment calls' of yours Squire?"

"Absolutely."

Silence followed for about ten minutes -- and then --

"Oh, Wilson."

"Yeah?"

"Six years."

"Huh?"

"I've been a Ranger for six years."

The trip was without incident. They approached the scene of today's battles expecting to find things as they had left them. Instead, they saw a small, almost welcoming campfire blazing.
~~~~~~~~

Wilson pulled up on his reins, matching the older Ranger. "Now, what do you spoze is goin' on, Squire?" he whispered, as both men unholstered their weapons.

"I don't rightly know yet, Son," said Daniels, scratching his stubbly chin. "Could be, that Kiowa got loose and built a fire, but I doubt he was strong enough yet. Seems to me we built that fire on the other side of that rock."

"I agree," whispered the younger man. "Might be Jacks, might be Witherspoon."

They walked their horses closer, scouring the perimeter of the campfire for any signs of life. When they were about twenty feet from the fire, a voice, unmistakably female, shouted from the rocks above, "Stop where you are! Now, throw down your guns!"

Wilson began, "Ma'am --"

But Squire shouted, "Miss Knight! Miss Knight, we're Rangers -- Squire Daniels and Wilson Tanner! We went up the mountain looking for you! We're back now to take you home!"

Suzanna scrambled down from the rock above them, ran to Squire, and, trembling, gave him a bear hug; then proceeded to the younger man with the same relieved emotion. An awkward Wilson squeezed the young lady back. In the ensuing embrace they both felt a release from the pent-up stress of the day. She covered his nose, his cheeks and finally his mouth with kisses of gratefulness; then realizing her actions, she pushed him back, looked at him, embarrassed, and apologized profusely.

Tanner, equally embarrassed, simply replied, "You're safe now, Ma'am."

She spotted the red hair beneath the top hat hanging from Squire's saddle, and stared for a long moment. Then she looked at Squire, a questioning look on her face. Finally she blurted out the question: "Why? Why bring that loathsome creature down the mountain?"

"Judgment call, Miss." The answer came from the young ranch hand, as Squire dragged the outlaw down from his horse and tied him securely to a small mesquite. Wilson continued, "Strictly a judgment call. Ol' Daniels, here, reckons 'tis the Christian thing to do – you know, shoot some fella, patch 'im up good, then if he moves, you can shoot 'im again."

Suzanna stood, horrified for an instant; then saw the twinkle in Wilson's eyes and the wry look of feigned disgust on Squire's, and frowned, trying to see the humor in the whole scenario. She could not; the rage was too deep.

"Ranger, you know he killed my father. He doesn't deserve to live." Then she turned her face away.

"Yes, Ma'am, I'm aware. He'll no doubt hang before long," Squire continued, without looking up.

Squire then moved to the horses. He looked after her horse and theirs, and then, as a final chore, went and checked on the Kiowa brave.

The young buck was awake, but in no condition to move. His bindings were still secure. Daniels tried to give him water to drink, but the Indian pursed his lips and turned away, the water spilling on the ground.

"Have it your way, Old Son," he said, and discontinued the attempt. He left the water pouch within easy reach, but took the weaponry. The Kiowa eyed him suspiciously.

"Just in case. You'll get it back tomorrow, as we're leaving," he assured the inexpressive warrior.

Back on their side of the boulder, Wilson and the girl were settled in for the night, the young lady curled up as she had been before the two rode in, and Wilson on the other side of the fire, his head resting on his saddle.

"Yessir," Squire laughed under his breath, packing his saddle a bit further away. "Helluva day."

Chapter 24

Indian Territory
Friday Early Afternoon
June 26, 1840

Drummer took the lead as he and Witherspoon got back to the muddy trail. They stopped just long enough to allow the ponies a quick drink. Drummer leaned over to inspect the hoof prints in the muddy ruts.

"Here's ours from this morning. See where we traveled up, then turned around and doubled back?" the young Ranger was explaining. Then he found what he was looking for

"Ah, here we are! Looks like the skittish one is Lottie's, see? It runs lighter than the others, and she tries to keep it reined in, to slow them down. That's why it keeps snakin' from side to side."

"Okay, Son. So they're headed back down the mountain toward Brisbie. Let's get after it, then, Drummer," Witherspoon breathed.

For the next half hour they rode at a gallop, then Drummer yelled, "Whoa! Whoa, boy!"

The ground had almost dried up to a trickle, but something about the tracks had changed in the past few minutes, and it didn't go unnoticed by young Hawkins.

"I didn't see nothin'. What you slow down fer?" Witherspoon demanded.

"One of the horses has lost a front shoe," the young tracker informed Witherspoon. "Look here, Jeb. He may have stepped on it with his back foot, or had it sucked off him when he went through a muddy rut."

Sure enough, Jeb could plainly see the cut marks in the soil from the unshod horse.

"That should make tracking them just a bit easier from now on!" He smiled, "An' they're gonna hafta stop once in a while to rest him, too, or he'll end up lame."

Ten or fifteen minutes later saw a tactic by Jacks which puzzled the two: the horse with no shoe left the trail, and rode the dusty western ridge some twenty feet above. After another few minutes the other two horses left the trail to the left, and continued parallel. At length, the three horses criss-crossed, still keeping company with the Brisbie road.

"What in hell?" questioned Drummer, "ain't seen nothin' like this before. Wonder what they're tryin' to prove?"

"Maybe they figure we'll spend a lot of time scratchin' our heads, an' in the meantime the sun goes down," surmised the older Ranger.

"Sounds about right," Drummer agreed.

It happened soon enough. The tactic was repeated twice more, each time the loop and criss-cross off the trail grew longer -- until finally the lone horse crossed to join the other two on the western side, and they didn't come back to the trail. Tracks showed they were moving at breakneck speed, south-southwest.

"They're not headed for Brisbie!" Drummer shouted, urging his filly onward. They're headed in a bee-line in the direction of Terros!"

Witherspoon shouted back, "Or mebbe that settlement old man Clarkston tried to get started on Silver Crick, that the Apaches burned out. Remember? Still a few buildin's last time I was through there."

"Don't think I ever been there!" Drummer called back. "All's I know, we got about two hours before we won't be able to see a blessed thing!"

They were in the Texas plains, losing precious daylight, with the possibility of running into a herd of bison or a Comanche war party, either of which would lessen their chances of finding the two remaining members of the Jacks' bunch or, as was much more critical, finding Lottie safe and sound.

"Got'em!" Drummer exulted, picking up the trail they had lost in the buffalo grass. "That one nag is puttin' up a fuss! Slowin' 'em down fer shore!" The two riders continued along the trail, now easily discerned by the erratic movements of the one horse and the missing shoe of the other.

~~~~~~~~
~~~~~~~~

Lottie Witherspoon sat her pony in silence, gag still in her mouth, but she had been chewing on it since the beginning of this trial, and by now had it just about chewed through. Her tongue could move parts of it around inside her mouth. Her jaw was numb with pain.

Lottie's pony had been a willing partner and confidante in the lady's plot. When Jacks' men had invaded her hotel room, she was in the process of putting on her finishing touches to greet the day. Her favorite brooch, about ready to be pinned on, still in her hand.

When the outlaws pushed her up to sit the saddle she had slipped that brooch under the saddle blanket. For the entire ride the pony had jittered and jolted with discomfort, but never bucked. At first, she'd done it to hide the valuable item, but now hoped it had been a useful tool for anyone tracking them.

~~~~~~~

Jacks and Buddy couldn't believe what they had just witnessed: that Ranger Witherspoon was still alive! "Not only that," Jacks spat out loud, as if in a stupor, "I've lost all my men except Buddy. Good men, they was! That Witherspoon! He must live a charmed life! I was sure I got 'im! But I never saw 'im fall. We shudda stuck around an' finished 'im off. I cudda got 'is badge. Damn! I shudda stayed an' got 'is badge."

Then to Buddy, "Damn, Buddy! We shudda stayed and got 'is badge!"

Buddy looked at his cousin in disbelief. "How many more you gotta collect before you're satisfied,
~~~~~~~

Maywell? Lissen! There's a good chance we can pick up a coupla new fellas in that ol' mining town up the road ten-fifteen mile or so. Or, hell! Mebbe we can join up with them!"

"We don't *ever* join up with some other gang, Buddy!" Jacks exploded. I want six good ...No! I want eight good men!"

Lottie rode on, listening to the two cousins bicker, chewing feverishly on the strings of cloth in her jaw, using her tongue to push the small bits to one side.

"Why, if we'd had more with us back in Brisbie this morning, Buddy," Jacks continued, "weed'a wiped 'em all out! Right across the street, they were! I'm tellin' you, Buddy, We're goin' to kill ever' lawman Texas turns out! We'll put the fear of God and Jacks in ever' corner of the Republic of Texas!"

"And when they put us at the top their most wanted outlaws list – maybe even put out some kind of reward for killin' us or bringin' us in, what then Maywell? I don't wanna die before my time."

"Buddy! What the hell's got into you? Didn't we decide we were goin' to destroy ever' lawmen we see for what they did to my Ma and Pa?"

"That's just it, Maywell. They was *your* Ma and Pa! An' that was a long time ago! I wanna have a wife to go home to someday! And some kids!"

"You chickenshit piece of scum!" Jacks was livid! "You backin' out of our deal? I ought to shoot your ass right now!"

"Aww, Maywell, eight years ago we was kids! When we made that deal Texas was wide open country. I never told you this before, but Pa told me he thought it was Comanche that burned you folks out. He said the only reason they had a badge was they must'a killed a lawman before they hit your homestead. You stuck to your story so hard, he just shrugged his shoulders and agreed with you."

"It was lawmen!" Jacks shouted. "Lawmen! They didn't scalp nobody, didn't do no screaming, the fellow with the badge -- tried to grab me – was wearin' a regular hat, an' he was a damn lawman! I ain't sayin' it again!" Jacks was almost in a rage at the challenge put forward by his cousin.

Oh No! Lottie thought, *Buddy's going to get himself killed! He is pushing Jacks to boiling over! I need to prepare for if and when that happens! Might not be a bad thing, though*, she reasoned. *If there's gunplay, let them shoot each other; so long as I'm not a target.*

"Anyway, Maywell," Buddy went on, "when we get to Silver Crick I think that's the end of the trail fer me. We can settle up there, I know you got some loot from the hotel we can divvy up. I'll prob'ly head on down south."

Buddy just wouldn't let go. He didn't seem to realize his cousin was going a bit haywire.

"Remember when we went all the way down to the ocean a coup'la years ago? I think that's where I'll head off to. Remember all the ships that came in there? I'm sure I can get a job there somewhere. Hell," Buddy laughed, "mebbe I'll become a Texas Range……"

Jacks didn't wait for Buddy to finish. His hand went to his gun. The shot dropped Buddy's horse, which by now was beginning to limp.

Buddy pulled his leg out from under the dead

animal, swearing a blue streak at his cousin.

"What the hell's got into you, Maywell?" the young outlaw bellowed. "You just shot my horse, damn you!"

"Here you go, Buddy!" Jacks reached in his saddlebag and pulled out two twenty dollar gold pieces, and dropped them in front of the bewildered, angry outlaw. "Couldn't let a lame horse suffer. You can figure out how you're gettin' to Silver Creek. Shoot ol' lady Witherspoon or ride double. Your choice. Maybe she'll keep you warm when it turns bitter cold tonight. But, so far as blood goes, we're done!" Maywell Jacks didn't wait for a response. He and his big, grey horse were gone!

Lottie didn't wait. She immediately wheeled her sorrel around in the direction they had come, and urged the mare into a full run. She knew she had rescuers following behind.

She could hear Buddy spouting a mixture of yelling, swearing and pleading. Then silence.

Finally in the distance she heard, "Hey Maywell! It wasn't no lawman! It was a Comanche! Ya hear me, Maywell? A Comanche!" Then laughing, and then nothing but her mare's hoofbeats.

With one final effort, Lottie Witherspoon tore through the last fibrous strings of the napkin from the hotel kitchen that had provided the gag used on her mouth. The cloth flew off her face to disappear in the dust behind. She spat and spat until the last remaining wads of napkin left her cheeks where she had been storing them. Her mouth was free!

"Jacob Witherspoon!" Lottie screamed at the top of her lungs. "I'm coming to you, Baby!"

Chapter 25

Brisbie, Texas
Friday, At Nightfall
June 26, 1840

"Didya hear? The Ranger and Big Kurt are back with those killers from this morning."

It was dark. Yet, news of their arrival spread around Brisbie even before they reached the sheriff's office.

Tom Lewis met them in front of his office. "Howdy, Kurt," the sheriff began, "I see you made it back okay. What about the others?"

"Oh, I expect they'll be along, Sheriff," Harlan Franklin interjected. "Squire Daniels is too cussed

to die, an' so long as he's okay, ain't no one else have the chance to leave this world afore their time!" A wry smile emanated from Harlan's face.

"We got three bad ones for you, Sheriff. One is wounded bad. Two are just fine."

"Yes, and we buried two more bad ones up in the hills," Franklin added.

"And the ladies?" asked the town sheriff. "Sounds like these fellas," pointing to the three still tied to saddles, "are most of the Jacks' bunch."

"Of the ladies we cannot say. Most of the others belongin' to the outlaws are, as you say, pushin' up daisies back in the hills," the blacksmith volunteered.

"Is Jacks dead?" Then not waiting for the answer to his first question, the sheriff asked a second. "And aren't these Indian ponies?" And then, "What's in those bundles?"

"Booty from the hotel. They never took it off their pony, an' we brought it back. Tom, stop askin' questions an' help us untie these three hombres, and get 'em in your cells," Harlan moaned. "This one here," he continued, pointing at Chester Smitts, "will need a real doctor. Squire saved him, but he sure as hell ain't no doctor. Man, Sheriff, I need a damn drink."

"Yes," agreed Big Kurt, "and my horse needs to rest – and so does my butt!" he added, laughing.

Sheriff Lewis emptied the one cell of its occupant, ushered the two outlaws into the cell; escorted Chester to a bench in front of the desk, where he willingly sprawled out, still in agony from the wound and the ride.

And finally, he turned to the previous cell occupant, George Chambers, "Go get Doc Barnes! Then get lost! An' don't come back, George!" he shouted, as he booted the rough-looking old drunk in the rear end. "I'm tired of feeding you Sunday breakfast!"

Turning to Harlan, Lewis smiled, "You don't know a thing about Squire Daniels! He's a better doctor than most in Texas. He went to medical school and just about went into doctoring. Only reason he didn't was so's he could fix up shot-up folks just to keep in practice."

"But, he fixed up a Kiowa and left him some water and the redskin's weapons. That ain't right, Sheriff. An', an' if he's so good, why'd you call fer this Doc Barnes?"

"Maybe so's Doc Barnes can learn sumthin'," Tom Lewis said, smiling.

"I'm done then, right?" Big Kurt Farber wanted to know. "I'll take the hotel stuff back, then take the horses over to the stable. Catch up with you boys tomorrow."

"And," Harlan added, "I'll fill out whatever reports you need, and walk you through everythin' we know, but right now I need to go to the nearest saloon and have a coupl'a stiff drinks."

Franklin tipped his hat to a bearded gent with a black bag as he walked out the sheriff's office and headed toward the nearest boisterous noises and laughter on the street. He walked through the swinging doors of the Wounded Buffalo and scanned the occupants at the various tables – a habit that saved his hide many a time since becoming a Ranger.

The first eyes that met his belonged to the drunk from the cell, George Chambers. The old codger was in tears, and being shoved around by three laughing cowboys -- cowboy to cowboy -- harassing him none too gently. From the looks on their faces, this was not an unusual event.

"Hold it right there, dammit!" Harlan yelled. "George, get your ass over here!"

"Who the hell are you, Mister?" one of the

three asked threateningly.

"Right Now, George!" Harlan yelled a second time, while pushing back his jacket to expose a star.

"Ah, hell, Marshal, we was just havin' fun with this old soldier, wasn't we Dan'l?"

"Ain't no fun in what you'all was doin'. I'm tired an' thirsty, an' I ain't killed no one yit today."

Gamblers stopped their card playing, the pianist stopped tickling the ivories and sat, hands at his side, and the Wounded Buffalo became suddenly very quiet.

Harlan continued, "Me an' your town blacksmith just brought in three members of the Jacks' bunch and tossed them in your jail. I don't want to throw any more of you'all in that jail, an' especially good law abidin' folks. Now, George here, has had just one drink shy of his last one for the day. You three show the kindness of law abidin' citizens and buy George, here, his last drink; then wish him Godspeed for the night!"

Then he turned to Chambers, who by now was standing at his side.

"You was a soldier, George? When?"

"Yes, Suh! Proud that I was, Suh!" the old man slurred. "I'ze a member of the Kentucky Rifles...last war with the Red Coats an' their Injun allies. Rank of Colonel. Wounded twice, but still kickin'," he grinned.

"I be damned! A hero! Right here among us, boys!" Turning to the three, by now sheepish cowboys, Franklin asked, "Any you boys got daddies that helped us stay free? No? Gents, I'll be around until the two missing ladies are back here. I'll be in here ever night, an' I want to see you three supply a few drinks for Colonel Chambers here. Are we all in agreement?"

As Ranger Franklin, his arm around the old soldier -- steadying him, walked slowly to the bar, the patrons gave them room. The bartender poured Chambers his last drink of the night. Then he pulled down a half-full bottle of his best whiskey from the shelf behind, and set it on the bar in front of the Ranger. The three cowboys gathered round him. Chambers shouldered his way next to them as well, but Harlan said sharply, "George, that was your last damn drink fer tonight! Now, skedaddle afore I walk you over to Sheriff Tom."

Then the Ranger poured each of the cowboys a shot from the bottle, watched the Kentucky Rifleman exit the establishment, then lifted his glass. They did the same.

"Number one, I ain't no Marshal. I'm a Texas Ranger." Then, "To George Chambers and Texas." The whole house echoed the sentiment.

Chapter 26

Southwest of Brisbie
Friday, Dusk
June 26, 1840

Drummer held his hand up for quiet. "You hear that, Jeb?"

"I hear nothin' 'cept the sun goin' down. Why? What you hearin'?"

"I expect it's a coyote, but it's a strange one," the young Ranger came back. "It came from directly ahead, but a long way away."

They rode on another quarter of a mile, until Drummer once again stopped.

"I heard it, too. That ain't no coyote. That's a woman yellin', and I think I know which woman it is." Witherspoon spurred his big white mare into a gallop, Drummer keeping pace. Both men pulled their weapons, but Jeb hoped guns wouldn't be required in this coming get-together.

Darkness was just inches away when they spotted her, far to the right of the barely visible trail created earlier by the trio. She would have passed them by, but as she rode, she was yelling something about her love for Jacob and could hardly wait to be in his arms.

Jeb squinted his eyes at Drummer, and nodding his head as if making a determined decision, said, "I think I'm gonna keep 'er, Drummer. You need to think about gettin' yerself one of 'em, too. They change yer whole outlook on life. I'm a changed man."

"Lottie!" the Ranger bellowed. "Lottie Witherspoon! Slow that pony down! Now! Dadgummit!"

Her sorrel's neck jerked back, as if in amazement, as horse and rider came to an abrupt stop. Jeb immediately raced to her, and flung his arms around her in a powerful, yet necessary embrace. He winced in pain from the hole in his left shoulder, but ignored it. Pain was irrelevant.

They clung together for what seemed to Drummer an eternity; then he sidled up beside them.

"We won't make it back to Brisbie tonight if you two keep on like that. Of course, we could stop here, set up camp and head back in the mornin'," he volunteered.

"Sorry, Drummer, but there are times," the old Ranger said, wiping the moisture from his eyes, "when nothin' matters, 'cept the feelin' of relief."

Looking into Lottie's eyes he continued, "This is one of those times."

"Jeb, untie my legs from this sweaty horse so I can get down and stretch for a minute," Lottie breathed. "I've been forced in this position for hours."

Once she got down, she walked a bit, exercised her torso and legs, then announced that she felt almost as good as new.

Then she saw the way Jeb moved his left arm, and saw, even in the darkness, the discoloration where a slight bit of blood had spotted through, and realized that her husband was in pain.

"Make camp right here," she decided. "We can start out early in the mornin' for Brisbie. Now take off your shirt, Ranger Witherspoon; let me see that arm!"

She proceeded to dab the wound with a wet piece of cloth torn from Jeb's shirt. As she did, she filled the Rangers in on her day's ordeal, then ended with the exchange between the cousins and her escape.

"Buddy is down the trail about, maybe two-three miles. He may have decided to walk toward that old burned out settlement on Silver Creek, but he'd have to leave all his gear behind. He certainly wouldn't pack it with him. He's probably still sittin' there beside that dead horse, cursin' his cousin, Maywell."

"Who knows where Jacks went off to. He's a bit possessed with the idea of destroyin' every Ranger or other lawman he sees. Buddy is nothin' like him."

Drummer, after listening to Lottie's tale, made an announcement: "You two set up camp; make yourselves comfortable. I'm goin' to get Buddy. Lottie, I'll be needin' your horse. Tomorrow you'll have to ride double with your hubby on that big white of his. Two-three miles you say? We'll be right back."

Lottie called out, "I don't think he'll mind at all; in fact, he'll be pleased to see you. Oh! Hold on a moment Drummer." She ran to the sorrel the Ranger was leading, reached under the saddle blanket, and pulled out the brooch. She held it up for Drummer to see. He only smiled, tipped his hat and rode off.

Jeb started a small fire using the fuel at hand; mostly dried buffalo droppings known to all as "buffalo chips". Then from his saddle bags he produced a small cache of jerky wrapped in a square of leather, a small tin pot with two tin cups inside it, and a leather pouch filled with ground coffee beans.

"I'm glad Drummer was thoughtful enough to leave so that I can take care of business," Lottie said laughing. She kissed Jeb on the lips, grabbed his shovel and rushed to disappear in the darkness. When she reappeared, she gave the camp her full attention.

"I dug a private latrine area over that knoll for tomorrow mornin'," she announced. "That way we can take turns doing 'the thing' without bein' embarrassed."

"So that's what took you so long. Next time sing out why you've been takin' so long."

While Jeb was shaking his head, smiling to himself and thinking: *leave it to a woman -- a fella wouldn't even bother about tomorrow morning's problems* -- Lottie was digging some "hip holes" to ease the discomfort of sleeping on the ground, making sure hers and Jeb's were separated from the two others.

The coffee pot sat on a flat rock over the flame. About the time the coffee was boiling, the two riders came into camp; Buddy with hands tied, sat astride Lottie's sorrel, the extra gear tied off behind him.

"Found him right where you left him," Drummer declared, "still sittin' on his dead horse, singin' that old song, what was it, Buddy?"

"The Gal I Left Behind," the outlaw moaned, embarrassed to be in Lottie's company.

"Thanks fer sendin' Drummer, here, back fer me, Mrs. Witherspoon. I don't know what I'd have done had he not showed up. Probably sat on that nag til he started to stink. I ain't proud of what me an' Jacks an' the others done, an' I know I ain't got much time left. I ask fer you to fergive me."

Witherspoon spoke up, "Ain't a one of us sayin' what's gonna happen once we git you back to Brisbie. Republic of Texas will make that judgment, Buddy. By the way, what's your last name, Buddy? Is it Jacks like your cousin?"

"Naw! Leibert."

"Why's your cousin so hell-fire agin' lawmen, Buddy Leibert?"

So, while they all enjoyed a minimal bit of nourishment and coffee, Buddy went through the history of the Jacks' family homestead massacre and the scars it left on Maywell's mental well-being.

"Time to turn in, Jacob," Lottie said. "We can finish all the discussions tomorrow in Brisbie."

Chapter 27

Palo Duro Canyon, Texas
Saturday Morning
June 27, 1840

Still dark! Suzanna raised herself on one elbow to look around. Squire was squatting over the fire, Crazy Red was in the exact spot Squire had dumped him the night before, and from the grimace on his face, in a lot of pain; Wilson was nowhere in sight.

"Morning, Ranger." The greeting came out strangely, as she was yawning at the time. Laughing, she apologized, as her hand flew back over her mouth to hide a second yawn.

"Don't apologize young lady." Squire could just barely see her outline as the sky became a little less black. "Yawning is good for you. Gets the blood flowing, and your lungs and brain working. It's like stretching the insides, you know, just like you stretch out your arms and legs."

Sun was sending fingers of pinkish-golden

hues on the rocks as Wilson came walking up from behind some boulders down the slope a bit, and acting like an embarrassed fool, mumbled a greeting to the young lady.

Squire pointed at the redhead, "Wilson, get that A-hole up and get him fixed up to go; I want to get started down this hill as soon as we can; we're still in Indian Territory."

"Miss, you should do the same. Come back refreshed, and we'll have a bite to eat. Wilson here brought along a few steaks he liberated from those Kiowa."

Steaks sizzled and coffee brewed on the mesquite fire. Suzanna watched them while Squire went to check on the Kiowa brave, and found him awake, and a little less belligerent. The warrior accepted a drink from the pouch, and took a strip of jerky from the Ranger.

Daniels tried to remove the Indian's bandages to inspect the stomach wound, but was rebuffed in his attempt. He shrugged his shoulders, shook his head, and walked back to the others.

Ten minutes later, "Okay folks," Squire said, "breakfast is over. Suzanna, do you mind riding with Wilson? Our prisoner is much heavier, and his riding double for a distance would be hard on my horse."

"I don't mind, Squire, but I was just getting to know and trust my horse: Courage. Wilson, would you mind riding double with me on Courage?"

Wilson laughed. "Naw, Miss Suzanna, I got no problems at all! Let's ride!"

Crazy Red was pushed up on Wilson's pony and tied to the horse's underbelly and pommel.

"Mornin', Blood Woman!" he grinned a big grin.

"Keep your filthy thoughts to yourself, you murderer! You killed my father, my friends my future! You have no right to live. I'm not sure why Ranger Daniels made the choice he did to bring you back to Brisbie; I just pray it's to put a noose around your neck in the town square, so that the Republic of Texas shows what happens to those who impugn rules, honor and fair play."

"Couldn't have said it better, Miss," Squire affirmed.

The three horses started down the slope; but Squire stopped in front of the fallen warrior. To the Kiowa, kneeling down, he offered the last of the prepared ram steak. Then, taking the knife he had set alongside the brave, he cut the bonds that held the warrior's wrists; next he thrust the blade in the ground beside the Kiowa.

The Kiowa then did something none of the whites expected. He grasped the knife, and slashed a line of blood across his palm; next, he indicated for Squire to stretch his hand out. Without hesitation, Daniels thrust his hand forward. The brave slit a line, drawing blood, across the Ranger's palm and pressed the two palms together.

Wilson, baffled, queried, "What the hell?"

"Blood brothers!" Crazy Red exploded. "I be damned, Ranger! You an' this Kiowa here are now blood brothers!"

"Wait a minute!" Red squinted in recognition. "I know you!" Red then growled a few words in the Indian's language. The warrior, in turn, laughed, and taunted the redhead with an obviously scornful remark. The exchange grew loud and long. Finally the outlaw had heard enough. He turned his face away, a trace of fear spread across his face, but the Indian wasn't through. It was plain to Squire that the warrior had threatened the redhead in some way.

Daniels mounted again, and as Crazy Red and the Kiowa again stared at each other, the four riders continued their journey toward Brisbie.

"What got you two so fired up at each other? What brought that on?" Squire wanted to know. "Oh,

that piece of turkey shit said he would soon boil my carcass over a Kiowa fire and feed my bones to the coyotes."

"Why? What'd you do him that riled him so?"

"Says I raped his bride-to-be."

Chapter 28

Almost forty miles to the southwest, another early morning camp was being broken up and its occupants preparing to ride toward Brisbie, Texas. Just like the other camp, this one, also, included two Texas Rangers, a lady and a prisoner. Even more strikingly, the prisoner here was also a captured member of the, by now, badly fractured Jacks' gang.

Drummer was the first to rise, stoking and adding fuel to the small fire. He put water on for coffee, woke Buddy Leibert up, watched as the prisoner took care of his morning needs, then sat enjoying a cup of coffee with Buddy as the husband and wife rolled out of their "bunk" and wiped the sleep out of their eyes.

"Drummer! Remind me to take you along whenever I hit the trail," Witherspoon smiled, grabbing the coffee pot. Lottie joined them for a couple of quick sips from the Ranger's cup, then announced she was ready to go – which, of course, meant that they were all ready to get on the trail back to Brisbie.

So once again this small group replicated the other, in that there were three horses, four riders. And, once again, the lady gave up her horse to the prisoner, and rode double with a man. The similarities far outnumbered the two differences in the two camps. But the two differences are worth noting: Lottie rode double in front of her husband, and Buddy Leibert was determined to be harmless, and so rode with only his hands tied to the saddle horn of his pony.

From different directions the two groups of riders headed for Brisbie, and interestingly enough, they reached their destination within the same hour in the early afternoon.

Only two hours too late!

Chapter 29

**Silver Creek -
Clarkston, Texas
Friday evening
June 26, 1840**

Maywell Jacks pulled into the remnants of the old mining concern on Silver Creek in the late afternoon. Since the fire, the town was usually deserted, but once in a while drifters came through to spend a few days before moving on. This day looked to be just an ordinary day.

"Damn it!" Jacks whispered aloud. "I was hopin' I'd get lucky!"

Slowly he walked the grey horse down what was left of the only street of what was once Clarkston, Texas, wondering his next move.

"Maybe I was a little too harsh on Buddy," he

continued, "maybe I should....."

"Step down off yer hoss!" a gruff shout came from the shadows of an old, mostly burned-out building. "Now, Mister! No funny stuff! Don't even think about reachin' fer yer weapon; my scattergun will send pieces of you all over both sides of the crick."

By the time Jacks dismounted and walked around the grey, there were four pairs of eyes staring at him from the doorway of that same building. Recognition came instantly to all.

"Jacks! Boys, it's Jacks! I'll be son-of-a-gun!" one of the ruffians expressed.

"Blue! Sonny! You're a sight fer sore eyes!" Jacks shouted. "Boy am I glad I run into y'all!"

"Last time we saw you was down in, where was that, Blue?" Navarro prompted.

"Galveston. That marshal, remember?" broke in Sonny. "Last year down in Galveston. Watcha doin' here in these parts, Jacks? Where's yer crew? That crazy red-head still ridin' with ya? Craziest som'bitch I ever seen!"

One by one Jacks answered each of their questions. Then they answered several of his. While they exchanged their stories, Jacks asked, "Where you hiding yore horses?"

"Inside," Blue laughed. "Didn't want anyone to know we was here."

They led him inside the big, empty, hulk -- which might have at one time been a saloon. Fire had destroyed most of the structure, including the bar. Most of the walls were charred, and a few half-burned arrow shafts were still sticking in various spots. Four horses were nervously prancing along the one still-standing wall.

"Apaches, I'm told," Jacks whistled. "I see yore still riding that Appaloosa, Chino," he remarked approvingly. "Good horse."

"You boys got plans? No? Good, cuz I got business to finish up in Brisbie!"

Navarro spoke up, "What you got lined up, Jacks? You still got a burr up your butt with lawmen?"

"My whole crew just got shot up by the law, an' you askin' me if it's just a burr? If I'd had you boys with me just this mornin', we'd have got rid of a bunch of 'em in north Texas.

No, boys! Listen up! Now, let me tell you what my original plans were. As you prob'ly know, Brisbie is the biggest town in Northeast Texas outside o' Witchita Falls. Well, me an' the boys rode into town to hit the bank and some other businesses. Figured there's only the town sheriff, so we'd take care of him, too." Jacks paused for effect. "What we didn't know until we asked around, was that about fifteen Texas Rangers were gonna have a pow-wow that day."

"Ha!' Blue breathed out. "That musta cramped your style."

"Matter a fact, we strung three of 'em up before we hit town; they was ridin' in from the northwest to be a part of that shindig – just happened to be in the right place when they came along."

"If you ride with me, we'll take the three saloons and the bank an' the general store. All the lawmen that were in Brisbie are probably still up in Indian country, all except for one who was trackin' me. But he wasn't really trackin' me. He was trackin' his wife, an' I had his wife. I left her back on the trail with my coward of a cousin, Buddy."

"You did what? You had a white woman with you and didn't keep her for company?" Chino was astonished. "She musta been real ugly! That's all I gotta say."

Jacks seemed to ignore the comment and continued, "You boys with me? We can go right now and hit Brisbie. I'm tellin' you, the town is ripe fer the takin'. No one would expect us to ride right back in and finish the job. And, Chino, if yore lookin' for a woman or two, we can probly find you a couple. They's gotta be eighty to a hundred folks there all told."

"Well boys, you heard Jacks. Do we throw in with 'im, or do we mosey on down to Waco or thereabouts?" Sunny asked. He looked around at the three faces staring at the newcomer.

Navarro asked a simple question: "So we ride along with you; what happens after?"

"Yeah," Blue chimed in. "You ain't my boss, Jacks! Me'n us boys, we ride together cuz we're friends; we stick together fer the same reason."

"I'm prepared to ride with you," added Chino. 'Then we divvy up the goods, ever one gets equal, and we ride in whatever direction we want. That's how I'll do it."

"Agreed! Let's ride."

As darkness began to settle over the dilapidated burned out remains of Clarkston, five horsemen saddled, crossed the little meandering stream called Silver Creek, and rode directly east, straight toward the bustling town of Brisbie, Texas.

139z

Chapter 30

**Brisbie, Texas
Saturday Morning
June 27, 1840**

Five men stepped down from their tired mounts in front of a horse trough; the morning was lovely. Huge cumulous clouds floating overhead at times hid the sun, causing giant shadows to meander along the main street.

Sonny reckoned it was close to 9 a.m. by the position of that sun in the sky. Chino walked to the pump handle and pumped water while the horses drank.

The whole town was a'swirl with a mixture of grief and elation: grief due to the murder of the town's own, and elation with news of the capture of members of the Jacks' gang.

The five walked into the *Copperhead,* asked a couple of bearded gents if they could sit, then pulled chairs out from the table and joined the two. Jacks then yelled to the barkeep for a bottle and glasses.

While they drank, they got everything they wanted from the two gents. *How many lawmen in town: Tom Lewis, the town sheriff; a Ranger, Harlan somethin' or another; and the blacksmith who was now a temporary Ranger. He's the one who helped Harlan bring in the Jacks' boys. How many? Three. They buried two up in the hills where the shoot-out took place. The others here in jail will be hanged prob'ly Monday or Tuesday. Sheriff said he'd wait til the other Rangers git back. There may be more for the rope.*

It was Saturday -- was the bank open? Oh, no! Marv Hightower wouldn't open on Saturday. But he'll be at the Good Night Hotel prob'ly right now, figurin' what its worth, because it looks like he'll be takin' it back over since Old Mr. Knight had a loan out, and well, now since Mr. Knight was gone and his daughter too, well....

"Much obliged fer yore company friends. Finish up the rest of the bottle; it's on us." Jacks smiled. And the five walked out of the *Copperhead*.

"Well, well. Looks like we just added to our outfit. Let's git on over and ask the sheriff real polite if we can have 'em back," Blue chuckled.

"I think I'd rather see which ones are over there," Navarro broke in, "before we spring 'em."

"My boys are all good boys!" Jacks went on, "I told you, I got rid of Crazy Red. I sent him up to the Kiowa camp. His red hair is hangin' from some Comanche belt by now."

"Okay, now at first, no shootin'! We take care of the sheriff, Tom Lewis with a knife or gun butt, but quick and silent. Then we go convince Hightower to open up his bank. Once we get that loot, we can throw some fear in everyone in town. Shoot the hell out of Brisbie. Hell, burn it down! Them people will throw all their valuables in the streets fer easy pickin's – Ha! Just like apples. Then we ride out, rich!"

~~~~~~~~~~

Tom Lewis sat behind his desk, smiled up at Blue and Chino as they walked in. "What can I do for you fellas?" he asked.

Blue peered behind Lewis to see that, sure enough, the jail cell was occupied by a few hollow faces sitting on wooden benches. He counted four. He walked to a corner away from the cell.

Meanwhile, Chino gave the sheriff a story about coming outside to settle an argument over the ownership of a horse that some feller said was his.

"We just got to town, Sheriff, and my friend rides an Appaloosa -- has done for six years; well, some old timer claims the horse is his and calls my friend a horse thief. We don't want no trouble, Sheriff, but unless you settle it, there may be gunplay."

Sheriff Lewis pushed his chair back and walked around his desk shaking his head and grabbing his hat.

"Damn! If it ain't one thing it's another! Where you fellas from?"

"Down south of here," Chino continued with his glib tongue. "Looking fer work. You know how that goes; but sometimes you get lucky. Any ranchers round here might need some summer help? Blue, here, is mighty good at tamin' the toughest
~~~~~~~~~~

broncs goin' and we're all good at workin' hard and keepin' our mouths shut."

Lewis turned to smile at Blue in time to see a gun butt crash into his forehead; he crumpled to the floor.

Quickly Chino found the cell key and swung open the door to the cell. The prisoners stood as if glued to the floor.

"Well, ain'cha comin'? Isaiah, Matt, you know us! Jacks is waitin' outside! Now we walk outta here like it's a nice day." Then he added, "No runnin' or shoutin' or makin' folks suspicious. Just walk reg'lar!"

Blue asked, "Where's your gunbelts?"

"He's got 'em locked up in that c-c-cupboard over there," Isaiah stammered, pointing to a small wooden cabinet. "Should c-clean it out of ammo, too."

"I don't think Smitty can make it," Matt observed, poking a thumb toward the man lying on the corner bunk, eyes staring in wonder at the commotion going on. "He was shot up bad up on the mountain," Matt told the two newcomers. "We should just leave him. He's been talkin' about dyin' anyway."

Chester Smitts tried to rise, but with a cry of pain he slipped back down to the cot. "Hell, yes! Just leave me! I shudda died yesterday. I was supposed to die yesterday. But I guess I can wait for the hangman. Tell Jacks I had a great time."

"Who's the old fella?" Blue wanted to know. "He with you?"

"Naw. This ol' boy's the town drunk," Matt volunteered. "Sheriff emptied him outta here last night, and then threw him right back in this mornin'. Now, what's the plan?"

Blue turned the floor over to Chino.

"We walk to the hotel you boys ransacked yesterday. Banker's over there, we understand, and we want to have a chat with him."

They dragged the sheriff behind the desk, pulled his badge off his chest especially for Jacks, and walked out the door, heading for the *Good Night Hotel.* Nobody bothered to close the cell door.

~~~~~~~

Marv Hightower was, indeed, in the hotel dining room when the seven men walked in. They explained the purpose of their visit, concluding with a proposal; Hightower was amenable to their proposal. The eight men walked... rather, strolled down the boardwalk. Hightower, with definite purpose: that of keeping his homestead out in Stoney Canyon from burning to the ground, and keeping his wife from being ravaged and strangled to death, and of course, keeping himself from watching that entire course of things happen before being blown away by a scattergun.

Navarro was the first to follow the elderly banker through the back entrance to the bank, the others followed closely behind. Matt elected to stay by the door in the event of trouble. There was none.

Hightower sat in a corner, head in his hands. After opening his office door and giving the outlaws the key to the big safe -- money box he called it -- they opened it, and the cash drawer inside. He could only think of the folks who had money in his bank, in that money box. Most were ranchers, farmers,
~~~~~~~

merchants ....

"And mine as well," he mumbled.

Heads jerked in his direction, and then turned away. Jacks threatened with a gun butt, then watched as the key turned in the lock.

Dear God, don't let them look too hard, he prayed silently.

Was he being punished for his greed? Marv winced at the thought. He didn't need to rush over to the hotel in such a hurry, did he? But with Brisbie being a growing center, that hotel would be a diamond to own. He was only thinking of their future.

A second mumble came from the banker, "Tess forgive me." Jacks swung his gun with full force. Marv Hightower wouldn't awaken.

"Where were we?" Jacks asked, looking down at the fallen banker.

"Nineteen U.S. silver twenty-dollar pieces, six fifty-dollar gold. Then there's a pile of Redbacks. Old man's got em in stacks of fifties. Must be twenty – thirty stacks; to round it off, there's another three hundred in Mexican pesos!" All this was counted and related by Navarro.

"B-b-boys, we're rich!" Isaiah exclaimed jubilantly. "How m-much is that apiece?"

Jacks said, "Including the Texas redbacks that's over three hundred each. I figure, by the time we get finished in the general store we're gonna have five hundred each."

"When w-we gonna split up the m-m-money?" Isaiah wanted to know.

Blue shrugged, "I'd say we leave here a couple at a time, out through the same way we came in."

From Chino, "Good idea. We should meet at the general store and take care of business before any of us start shootin'."

"Hold on, Jacks," Matt said. "There's a couple of Rangers that knows Isaiah an' me. If we run into 'em in the general store, well, I'm shootin' first!"

"Understood."

"B-but when we gonna split up the m-m-money?" Isaiah was more adamant.

Navarro, disgusted, almost shrieked, "What's this old m-m-man's c-c-c-cut, J-J-Jacks?"

From a sheath somewhere behind him, Isaiah pulled a hunting knife and sliced Navarro's neck before the man could twitch an eye.

No one spoke. The three outlaws, Chino, Blue, and Sonny, men who had ridden together for years, looked at each other in abject shock. Swells of hatred filled the banker's office at the stuttering, grizzled old fool that had just killed their comrade.

Jacks said in very calm tones, "Boys, a big mistake was made just now. Isaiah, I'm sorry Navarro teased you like that, an' I'm even more sorry it ended like it did. Sonny, Chino, Blue – we need to keep cool heads. Now is no time to go fightin' among ourselves. We're in the middle of the biggest haul yet; let's finish it. We can ride to the banker's place out in Stoney Canyon. He gave us directions, remember? We'll split the loot there and then we can go our own way."

No one else had a word to say. Isaiah seemed satisfied; the three remaining friends of Navarro were decidedly not.

~~~~~~~

Harlan Franklin was sitting at Kurt Farber's
~~~~~~~

blacksmith shop while Big Kurt was at the bellows, pounding out and forming a piece of red hot iron in the forge. They were going over the events of yesterday. It was already after 10 a.m.

"Too bad we didn't get Jacks," Harlan said. "He could be a thorn in our sides if he's allowed to remain on the loose."

"Yeah," agreed Kurt, but we buried some and brought a few back here. I think I'll have a job soon building a gallows. Tom hasn't asked yet, but ..."

"I think," Franklin interjected, "he's waitin' to see who else comes in with Witherspoon and Squire. Could need a bigger gallows," he laughed. "So, Kurt, what do you think about becomin' a full-fledged Ranger?"

"Oh, I don't know, Harlan. I've got work lined up for a couple of months; in fact I could use a helper. Brisbie keeps growin' and if Texas gets statehood, this country will boom. We already have a lot of immigrants comin' in from Kansas and Nebraska. I think I'll stay right where I am."

"I thought you'd say that," Harlan smiled. He looked up to see a familiar figure half stumbling, half running toward them from a distance.

"Ranger Franklin! Kurt! Come quick!" George was almost screaming as he stumbled along.

"Oh, here comes Chambers. Ha! ... Hey, what's goin' on George? Our Ranger boys back in town?" Franklin called out.

Big Kurt chuckled, "Ol' Chambers sure took a likin' to you, Harlan. Really a good sort; too bad he drinks so much."

"Yeah, spends half his time in the Wounded Buffalo and other half livin' over there in a jail cell with Tom; matter of fact, he musta just got out."

The old Kentucky Rifles regiment member was nearly out of breath when he reached the two Rangers.

"Jailbreak! Sheriff Tom's been kilt! Ya gotta come. Some real bad ones. They..."

Harlan didn't wait to hear the rest. He ran down the main street in the direction of the jailhouse, Kurt and George shuffled behind, the blacksmith pumping questions into the old man's brain --

How many? Did he know any of them? Where were they headed? For each question there was no answer except, "I don't really know. I was just soberin' up, an' it's all mixed up in my head. All's I know is the sheriff's dead, that one wounded fella says he's gonna die, and they left the cell unlocked, so I come to get you. I knew I'd find you both down here, so I got here fast as I could."

"You did fine George, you did just fine," Big Kurt assured him.

The big man then made a decision --wheeled and ran toward the stables to fetch the Rangers' horses. He threw saddles on both in a hurry, and rode one out, leading the other. George stood in the entry of the stables scratching his head, then ran to the corral behind the stables to get his own steed.

In the meantime, Harlan had already reached the sheriff's door. He pushed it open. Sheriff Tom Lewis lay sprawled behind his desk, his head in a pool of blood, his boots sticking out in the open.

Still in a corner of the open cell, Chester Smitts struggled to sit up. He was sobbing.

Harlan, hands on his knees was trying to

catch his breath, taking in great gulps of air while assessing the scene before him. The small, familiar weapons cabinet had been ripped apart; a few pistols were on the floor, but the two shotguns and all the 12 gauge buckshot Tom kept in that lockup were missing.

Harlan walked inside the cell, knelt down in front of Smitts. "Who was it, Smitty?"

"Didn't recognize them at first, but then I remembered." Smitty's face was contorted with pain from his gun wound, and was struggling to hold back tears – "they was runnin' with Jacks an' us last year down south. A fella named Blue...." The outlaw gave in to the pain, and he stopped to catch himself. "Ranger! Damn! Just a minute!" He held his hand up, as a wave of pain shuddered through his entire frame, before continuing. "I hurt so bad! Oh, uhhh, the other one's Chino."

Franklin stood and pursed his lips. "Jacks' buddies, eh? You don't suppose......" he spoke basically to himself.... Then, "Why did you come into town yesterday, Smitty?"

"We needed some money, and Jacks wanted to kill another lawman or two. Only reason we left the hotel in such a hurry was cuz we heard they was fifteen lawmen in that ....." another grimace and moan from Smitty, "....that saloon across the street; too many of 'em to take on."

"Okay, Smitty, I gotta run. I'll have someone get the Doc, and send him over. We'll just leave the cell open for him; you ain't goin' nowhere."

He turned, put his hand on the door to push it open when he heard the first blast from the scattergun. Quickly he threw himself prone on the floor of the office and pushed the door wide open. Another blast from the smoothbore scattered shot through the doorway over his head.

Harlan, lying on the wooden floor, with colt in hand, put two shots into the shooter and another into the man's companion. Both men dropped in front of him, staring grotesquely at him in wonder, from only five or six feet away. The shooter was no longer moving. His companion tried to recover and direct his weapon at Harlan, but another shot from the Ranger's weapon ended his attempts.

Out in the street, he recognized his own pony, reins dragging in the dirt. Another, rider-less mare was limping alongside, with her rump bloody and torn. Her rider, or what was left of him, was lying in a pool of blood.

Harlan ventured cautiously into the street, crouching low. He scanned left, then right. He watched as several riders scuttled out of town; one was riding an Appaloosa.

Town folk came running from everywhere; a blanket was produced to cover Big Kurt's body. Youngsters kept multiplying, coming from every direction to see all the excitement. By the time Harlan had determined the streets were safe, the crowd was above forty, including a very sober, very upset George Chambers.

"Who's in charge here?" Harlan yelled. He held his hand up for quiet. Most quieted down; only the unruly children were, like children everywhere, ignoring the adults. Finally, ears were twisted, behinds were swatted until a semblance of order was attained.

"Look!" Harlan yelled, once he could be heard,

"We've had a catastrophe here in Brisbie. We lost the town sheriff; we lost the town blacksmith, and we lost the hotel owner. We need to pull together in an organized fashion. Is the Doc here? Do we have a mortician in town? Step out if you're here."

Doc Barnes elbowed his way to the front, and with him came Milton Sanders, the mortician.

"You two fellows do your own organizin'. You'll find Tom Lewis layin' inside. You'll be steppin' over those two," he said, pointing at the two ruffians lying almost inside the sheriff's door, "and of course, Big Kurt out there in the street."

"They need to disappear pronto! We don't need a bunch of kids and others gawkin' at the dead. Now the two outlaws in the doorway – drag 'em in to have Chester take a look at them. He can identify who they were. He rode with 'em all. Now, unless you have some information for me – anythin' I need to know about -- the rest of you, go on home. We've had enough killin' fer one day!"

The Brisbie main street was quickly emptied except for those who were appointed to carry the dead to the mortician's workshop, the Kentucky Rifleman, and a couple of grizzled old cowboys.

Chester Smitts identified the dead outlaws as Matt, one that Harlan and Kurt had just brought in the day before, and a newcomer, Sonny. That meant Jacks was still alive.

"You boys got somethin' to say?" Harlan asked the two old hangers-on.

"Well, Ranger, don't know if it means anythin'," one of them started, "but them two was some of 'um that sat in *The Copperhead* with me'an Bill, here."

"Yeah, an' they was askin' lots of questions 'bout the general store an' the banker," Bill put forth.

"So what'd ya tell 'em?"

Bill looked at the other fellow, Wally, who shrugged his shoulders and said, "We didn't say nothin'. They was really nice, wasn't they Bill? They even left us a bottle they'd bought."

"How many were there?"

"Oh, I guess four or five. Wally looked back at Bill for confirmation."

"They's five of 'um. I 'member cuz they had to drag an extree chair over from another table."

"Thanks fellas. An' yore sure you didn't tell them anythin' about the banker or maybe the layout of the general store?"

"Naw, oh! They asked if the bank was open an' Wally said, 'whoever heard of a bank open on Saturday'! We told them 'ol man Hightower was in town, though. But that's okay isn't it? I mean, to say Mr. Hightower is here in Brisbie?"

"How did you know that, Wally?"

"He came in early an' Alice poured him a cup a coffee. Sat right there at the table next to us. Alice asked him what brought him into Brisbie, an' he said he was goin' over to the hotel 'cross the street. He laughed and said he was goin' to get a value on it."

Bill joined in, "May hafta sell it to pay the bank back, is what he said."

Harlan's brow furrowed. "And did you tell those five gents all this?"

"Yes."

"Shit!" Harlan spat out. He kicked one of the empty chairs. "Shit!"

Chapter 31

Somewhere between
Wells and Brisbie, Texas
Noon
June 27, 1840

Three men were pushing their horses at a gallop straight for Brisbie: George Birdwell, Jess Blackman, and Ollie Taylor, all Texas Rangers.

Jacks and his gang of thugs had to be stopped for good. Birdwell was determined. Had he known that three of his detail had been hanged, that Tom Lewis the local sheriff and temporary Ranger, Kurt Farber had also fallen to the Jacks' crew within the last 48 hours he would be even more furious.

Brisbie would be the headquarters of an all-out manhunt for the killers. Texas could and would not tolerate this vermin to remain free!

Chapter 32

Brisbie, Texas
Saturday Morning
June 27, 1840

The sun overhead indicated it was crowding noon. Harlan walked slowly into the sheriff's office. Doc Barnes was leaning over Smitts putting some ointment on the man's wound.

"Did Tom make it?" Harlan asked, looking hopefully at the doc.

Doc Barnes sadly shook his head before answering. "Nope, I'm afraid Tom's dead. They stripped his badge off'n him, too. I guess it's that Jacks' bunch alright."

"I need some men. When you got a minute, write me out a list of three or four good ones. We're gonna wipe that son-of-a-bitch off the face of Texas."

George Chambers stood close by, listening. "I'm one of 'em, Ranger. Don't confuse my drinkin' with my ability to shoot what I aim at."

"Okay, George. Let's you'n me run over to the bank an' check it out. We'll be back in a bit, Doc. George, have you ever broke into a bank before?"

"Been awhile."

Doc Barnes smiled grimly at the conversation as he sat to write out a list of what he deemed a good selection of competent men to assist the Ranger in his pursuit of the Jacks' bunch.

The two men reached the bank and found the front entrance secure. They walked to the rear door. It, too, seemed locked up tight, but there were recent boot prints all around in the dirt.

While Harlan was assessing them, George backed up to the door and planted his right boot against it with full force. The hinges gave way and the jamb splintered. The two men entered, Harlan frowning at the tactics used.

"I could arrest you right now, Old Man!" he snapped.

"Fer what, Ranger? We needed to get in, didn't we? You said it yerself. You didn't have no key, did you? Now we're in, ain't we?"

"Breakin into a ban..... Ohhhh, She-it!"

Now inside, they had reached the banker's office door and the scene wasn't pleasant. Two men lay on the blood-covered floor.

"This here's Marv. I don't know the other'n," the Kentucky Rifleman said.

"What do you make of this, Ranger?" Chambers asked, pointing at what looked like some

attempts at markings made by the banker's finger through the puddled blood.

"Hmmm, I don't know, George. I didn't even

see it, but I think yo're right. He was tryin' to write somethin'. Looks like an X and two squiggles. Run, get Doc Barnes, George, while I take a look around."

"Right, Ranger."

Careful not to disturb the probable last written thoughts of the banker, Harlan opened drawers and cupboards, walked through the entire small structure, pulling out a cashier's drawer to reveal a handful of redbacks.

He pulled a lift-out insert from the drawer, underneath was a ledger sheet, showing five dollar payouts to the local Rangers: Squire Daniels, Jacob 'Jeb' Witherspoon and a new heading for Drummer Hawkins with nothing yet noted in the column.

Going back into Hightower's office, Harlan took a closer look at the built-in safe. It was wide open and empty, a few papers on the floor – some blood-soaked. Taking a closer look at the safe itself he discovered it had a false back.

"Clever!" Harlan whistled. A couple of small holes just large enough to poke a finger through. He did. The grey metal sheet came out of the safe. Behind was a wall composed of three columns of small numbered wooden compartments, twenty-one in number, each of which had a lock. Below the compartments was a wider, locked drawer. The Ranger whistled again. All were locked. Carefully, he put everything back as he found it.

Doc Barnes and Chambers appeared in the doorway, along with the mortician.

"Thought we'd just as well bring Sanders along. He's gonna haf'ta get in here sooner or later," George murmured. "Either of you two figure this out?" pointing at the squiggly marking on the floor, left by the banker. "Not a clue," Doc Barnes said, frowning at the markings.

"Me either," agreed the mortician, looking around, more interested in the dead men lying on the floor. He got eleven dollars for each body he took care of, and today was one of his best days ever.

The men picked the two up and carried them out the back way. Once outside, Harlan checked the clothing of the deceased for any valuables or papers of importance. That's when he found the small key.

"This must be for the drawer under those compartments," he mused aloud.

Chapter 33

Brisbie, Texas
Saturday Noon
June 27, 1840

The other man was one of the killers; gonna have to bring Chester Smitts over here to identify this one, Harlan thought. While he was considering the dead outlaw, Squire Daniels appeared; on Squire's heels was Wilson Tanner.

"We've been in town for about fifteen-twenty minutes," Squire informed Franklin. "We heard most of the news. I don't think anyone is aware of this mess," he shook his head pointing at the two laid out on the ground.

"Got some more business for you, too, Milton," Wilson announced to the mortician. "We walked through the hotel with Suzanna, and found a dead fella in room twenty-eight upstairs. I guess he was a federal surveyor name of Samuel Hardy from New York or somewhere back east, stateside. Had his throat slit. Nobody thought to check the rooms yesterday morning."

"So, you know we lost Big Kurt," Harlan stated.

"They'd a got Harlan here, too, but this is one smart Ranger." George Chambers took over the explaining. "Why, he threw hisself to the floor and shot two of 'em while he was flat on the ground. If he'd a bin standin' he'd a had a hole in 'im big as one a' Alice's apple pies."

Wilson Tanner introduced Chambers to Squire. "George, here, can usually be found at one of our local waterholes. Whenever we come into town for a drink or some dancin', he's usually holdin' the bar up. What're you doin' here George?"

"I'm thinkin' on joinin' up with the Rangers. Action is my style, an' there's a fair bit goin' on. Now thet me'n Harlan seem to know each other's mind, I figure we make a good team."

"That'll be up to George Birdwell, George. And while I'm thinkin' on it, if you become a Ranger, we gotta change yore name. Can't have two Georges. I think we'll call you Kentucky. Has a good ring to it," Harlan smiled. "But listen, Kentucky! Drinkin' is comin to a halt! If we're pards, we walk into the bar together, we drink together, and we walk out together. Sober! You agree?"

The Kentucky Rifleman spit in his hand, held it out for Harlan to grasp. Harlan spit in his own and complied.

The six men returned to the main street carrying the two deceased. As they were walking to the mortician's workhouse, another score or more townsfolk came from their businesses or shopping. Cries of anguish and sorrow erupted. Within the last thirty-six hours, their hotelier, their sheriff, their town blacksmith, and now their banker -- all murdered. A strange sight: walking into Sander's workshop, seeing the men laid out on the floor, Wilson shook his head and cursed.

Squire suggested they return to the sheriff's office to exchange information, but when Wilson reminded him that Crazy Red was now behind bars in the jailhouse, he changed his mind.

"Let's go over to *The Good Night* instead."

"How's Suzanna?" Harlan asked. "Sure good seeing y'all. We were worried about you when you said you was goin' up that mountain after the girl."

"We got riders comin' in from the south!" Kentucky announced, peering out the hotel window. All those in the room went to the front door, guns drawn.

"It's George. Couple Rangers with him," said Harlan. "How'd he know Jacks was here, I wanna know!"

"You'll have a chance to ask 'im in a minute." He walked outside and motioned for the riders to come to the hotel. Once inside they decided to proceed to the dining hall. More room in there, and they could pull chairs around a table and all sit together. After introductions all around, and the latest in the list of atrocities related to the newcomers, the territory manager took over the meeting.

"I want Jacks and I want him sooner than later!" George Birdwell shouted, slamming his fist on the table top. "We know he picked up some new fellows, and we know he was here just this morning." He looked around the room and finished with an emphasized, "Again!"

Kentucky figured it was his turn to speak. "Five came in, picked up two from the jail, lost three in fights here in town, which leaves four. Now…"

"Right!" spat Birdwell, glaring at the old fighter. "Now, just who are you, again?"

"Me? I'm George, uhhh, Kaintucky Chambers, at your service, Sir. Figure on joinin' up with you Rangers."

"That right? Well, Mr. Chambers, in these parts, I decide who gets to be a Ranger and who doesn't. You understand?"

"Yes I do, Sir."

"Good. Tell you what, Mr. Chambers. You go find Suzanna, ask her if she would be kind enough to whip up a pot of coffee and maybe some cookies if she has any hiding anywhere. Meanwhile, I have a few questions to ask Harlan here about your potential qualities as a Ranger." Turning to Wilson he said, "You go with him. We may as well assess you as well; that is, if you want to become a Ranger permanently."

"Thinkin' about it," Wilson grinned, and walked out with the older fellow.

No sooner had they walked out than Kentucky poked his head back through the door.

"We got four riders comin in from the north! One looks like Witherspoon's horse."

"Good! Good, now go find Suzanna."

Chapter 34

Brisbie, Texas
Saturday Afternoon
June 27, 1840

Wilson walked outside and waved the Rangers to the hotel.

"Had a repeat visit from Jacks. We got hit bad. Banker's dead, Tom Lewis, an' Big Kurt, too. They pulled their boys outta jail, you know, Isaiah and Matt. Chester was too hurt to join 'em. Anyway, Harlan got two of 'em. That Matt fella, and one called Sonny. An' then to top it off, they musta had a fight 'tween themselves, cuz one of 'em ended up with a slit throat. None of us did it, an' we don't know who it is."

Witherspoon took in all the information matter-of-fact, pursed his lips, and spat.

"Good man, Tom." And then, "Lottie, slide

down offen this white nag so's I can git down a bit easier. Go on inside. I'll be right there."

"Drummer take Buddy, here, over to the jailhouse and lock him up. Then kindly take our horses to the livery; grab these other three nags and run 'em over there, too. Then come on back. I'll have Lottie git a pot a' coffee goin'. Sure hope Suzanna's here. I forgot to ask Wilson." The Ranger then walked up the steps, into the hotel, and poked his head in the dining hall where he was welcomed by a crowd of lawmen.

Birdwell started in again. "Gentlemen, we have a job to do before we go home. We have, what seven of us here, eight if we include Kentucky. What's his real name Harlan?"

"George, George." Harlan laughed. "He was a member of the Kentucky Rifles in the War. Rank of Colonel. Drinks a fair bit, but I think we came to an agreement, an' I think he'll be a good addition."

"Squire, what about Wilson?"

"Wilson is a good man," Daniels affirmed. "But I have a thought that just came to me when I learned about Brisbie's losses. Town needs a sheriff with Tom gone. I think everybody in town would vote for him, and if he agrees, I think we could make it official by tomorrow."

Suzanna and Lottie had been talking in Suzanna's office off the dining room. Suzanna had been sobbing, you could see the watery eyes and tear stains still on her cheeks. But like the trooper she was, she lead the way into the kitchen, where she and Lottie prepared some beef sandwiches and a pot of coffee for the group.

George called in Wilson and Kentucky.

"What's your full name, Kentucky? And what year were you born?

"George Washinton Kaintucky Chambers, born year of our Lord, 1784, Sir."

"Now then, raise your right hand, Colonel George Washington Kentucky Chambers."

So, at the age of fifty-six, Kentucky became a Texas Ranger right then and there.

"Now as your first duty as a Ranger, go get Doc Barnes, and the mortician, the general store owner, Alice from across the street, and the town preacher -- bring them here, pronto."

Chambers ran from the hotel. In the meantime, the men discussed what had transpired during the last two days.

"I just want to recommend we buy all them colt revolvers we can," Harlan Franklin commented. "I put three bullets in two of them fellers quick as a wink. I'd a'been dead if I'd a'been usin' my old pistol."

All the Rangers nodded or made approving um-huhs, and Witherspoon added, "Turned back the Kiowa, let me tell you. They couldn't figure how we could shoot without reloadin'."

"That's good to know," Birdwell smiled. "I'll pass that on to HQ, an' I'll requisition more. Are you happy with the rifles, too, or just the pistols?"

"Everthin' worked just fine. Didn't have no jammin' or nothin'!"

Lottie came to the table with a plate of sandwiches, Suzanna right behind with coffee; a brief respite took place. Wilson noticed Suzanna's face; he reached for her hand as she passed by, and asked if she was alright. She smiled a brave smile, and squeezed his hand before carrying on.

New faces showed up in the dining room: Alice came first, then Jenkins the preacher, Harold the general store owner, followed by the Doc, the mortician and Kentucky entering together – all with questioning faces.

"Come join us," George Birdwell invited with a sweeping arm.

"Sit. Have a cup of coffee. We may have left a sandwich, but make sure you leave one for Kentucky, here," he smiled pointing to the newest Ranger. "We need to go through a few things with you leaders of Brisbie. My authority goes so far, but I can't step on your toes."

So while the newest of the participants were enjoying a cup of coffee, George started talking about the character of a Ranger: that he needs to be solid, of good reputation, not a drunk, not a liar, respectful, and a few other qualities. George ended up by saying they had decided Chambers had the "stuff" but then they suggested that Wilson also had the qualities. The Double Bar S cowboy showed skill and diligence in the midst of the recent troubles, and they were considering offering him a permanent Ranger position if the cowboy agreed.

The town folks nodded their heads in unison, as Birdwell sipped his coffee. Wilson smiled and murmured that he was willing.

"Okay, folks.... I'm going to have Squire continue."

Squire, stayed seated. He eyed Wilson and smiled. "Wilson, the Rangers need good men; but this town needs a good man to be its sheriff." Then turning to the town leaders, he continued, "Folks, I

8

propose, we elect Wilson Tanner as our new Brisbie sheriff."

The room immediately erupted in cheers. Wilson looked sheepish as Squire pinned a badge on his chest and had him swear an oath to keep law and order in the town of Brisbie.

"No more riding broncs and chasing maverick steers, Cowboy!"

Wilson looked up to see the first smile he had seen all afternoon on Suzanna's face.

"Well, folks, I think I can do a fair job. I'm not Tom Lewis, and I'll need a few of you Rangers to help me learn some basic stuff, but I'll do my best. As my first objective, I want Jacks and his crowd in the town square standin' on a gallows."

"Agreed. Did anyone in town see which way Jacks went?" Birdwell asked.

"No, the four or five of 'em rode out north, but split up as soon as they hit the outskirts and all went in different directions," the general store owner volunteered. "They definitely planned that move."

"One of 'em rode a nice piece a' horseflesh," Harlan added. "An Appaloosa."

"Anythin' else?"

"Might be nothin," Kentucky offered, "but Hightower was tryin' to write sumthin' whilst he was layin' on the floor in the bank."

"How was that? What do you mean, writing?"

"In the blood! It was all around him, an' he used his finger, I 'spect."

As the womenfolk cringed, Squire said, "It might be nothing, but just the same, let's have a look."

Meeting over, the people returned to their places of business. Witherspoon, Squire, and Wilson, along with Kentucky went to inspect the floor of Marv Hightower's office.

"See here? Looks like a big X an' then a coupla kinda, snakey lines or cricks or sumthin'. Harlan called 'em squiggles or sumthin' like 'at, but we couldn't figger it out."

"Anyone go out to Hightower's ranch an' let the Missus know Marv was killed?" Wilson asked, as an afterthought. "Maybe one of the fellas should ride out and let her know she's a widow."

Witherspoon said, "Yeah, I'll go. I know where the Hightower spread is, and I know Tess. I'll take Lottie with me. She'll help Tess make it through the news. What a damn shame."

"Anybody got any ideas what this means, if anything?" Squire asked, pointing to the markings in the puddled blood. "Possibly just uncontrolled reactions – twitching or such as he lay dying – and you're right, a damn shame."

"Nope! That's writin!" the old Colonel was adamant. "I guarantee!"

"Now, what's the town gonna do for a banker?" Wilson changed the subject, scratching his head. "Jimmy Mann will have to step up and fill Marv's shoes, I reckon."

"Maybe someone should ride over to Wichita Falls and pull a banker in from there, temporary or permanent, to give Jimmy a hand." Again, this was Squire.

"Birdwell ain't too awful far from there," spoke up Witherspoon. "We can ask him or one of his boys to ride on over and recruit someone."

"I don't think Suzanna will have any problems at the hotel," Squire observed, "once the shock and sadness part of her ordeal is over. The way she handled herself on that mountain would make any man proud to have her as a partner."

Squire took a sidelong look at Wilson, who immediately blushed full red, then angrily said, "I just met this girl! You talk like we're gettin' hitched by Pastor Jenkins tomorrow mornin' at the church house!" Then he laughed at a thought. "Wait til I catch my breath and have been sheriff for a week at least."

"Well, lad," Jeb grinned, "you walked in the hotel, just a young buck of a cowboy, and you walked out, the sheriff; mebbe, though, come to think of it – mebbe you should stay away from goin' to church for a coupla weeks."

"You don't take her on, I just might!" Kentucky offered. The four burst into hearty laughter.

"Best we get on back to the others," Witherspoon said. "We all have some thinkin' to do about how to proceed in findin' Jacks."

Chapter 35

Brisbie, Texas
Saturday Afternoon
June 27, 1840

Drummer took Buddy from the jail, walked him over to the mortician's workhouse, showed him all the bodies lined up and asked him to identify the dead outlaws.

"This one is Matt. If I remember rightly, his last name is Bingham. These other two are part of a bunch we rode with down south last year. This fella here is Sonny and this one is Navarro. Looks like Navarro got mixed up in a private quarrel with one of his pals. Don't know any last names. Huh! They musta been in Silver Crick; we was headed there when Jacks 'n me split up. Them boys, Sonny and Navarro, rode with a feller name of Blue and one called Chino. Chino rode a mighty pretty horse; it had a spotted rear end."

"He was one of 'um," Drummer said. They walked back to the jail.

"Sorry about your sheriff," Buddy said.

"Right. Let me ask you this: we buried two up on the mountain. Since you see everyone here or in jail, who did we bury?"

"Well, Boo fer one. He's just a kid...sixteen, I think. Last name? Uhh, it'll come to me in a minute. The other'n was Bobby Epps - one mean ol' son of a bitch. He needed dyin' if anybody did. Why do you need the names? They're dead. Ain't gonna bother nobody no more."

"Record keepin'. Down in Houston they keep records on everythin'. I think killers, whether Indians or the likes of you have to be documented. Your names will go in the Houston Star or some newspaper, so that ten years from now, somebody, perhaps an old, sad mother will say, 'Can you please tell me, what ever happened to my son, Henry *Buddy* Adamson?' The newspaper people who keep the records will look it up and say, 'Oh, that son of a bitch was hanged in Brisbie back on July 1, 1840.' Do you see, Buddy?" Buddy swallowed, and failed to respond.

"When you think of Boo's name let me know."

"I don't think I will now, Ranger."

~~~~~~~~

Wilson deputized six able-bodied men, men that were recommended by the mortician and the doc; so with them added, the lawmen now numbered fourteen. The plan was to ride to the outskirts of Brisbie, take readings of hoof prints north, south, east and west, to see if any were consistent in ultimately heading toward a particular destination
~~~~~~~~

or at least, in a particular direction.

Heading toward Stoney Canyon
Saturday Afternoon
June 27, 1840

In the meantime, Witherspoon and his wife, Lottie, headed southeast toward Stoney Canyon to break the news to Tess that her husband of thirty years had fallen victim to outlaws.

They had ridden about five miles along the grassy, buggy trail, when Jeb stopped the big white mare. He stared at the ground.

"What are you lookin' at, Honey?" Lottie asked anxiously. "Somethin' wrong?"

Witherspoon pointed at the ground. The banker's carriage wheel tracks were plain enough in the ruts, but fresh tracks lay on top -- horses -- heading toward the ranch.

"What should we do, Jeb?"

"*We* shouldn't do anythin'. I want you to head to Brisbie in a hurry and get the crew. I think the Jacks' gang is holed up at Hightower's place."

"Jeb Witherspoon! Stoney Canyon is only two or three more miles! Every minute counts. Goin' back five miles and then comin' back again is twelve to thirteen miles of ridin'. I'm stayin' here with you!"

"Lottie, yore talkin' nonsense now! I don't have a problem goin' up against three or four, but it would be easier with ten of us against four of them!"

"And Tess may be dead – or worse – before I get to Brisbie. Jeb, give me one of those colts!"

"Lottie, you've gone compl..."

"Give me one of those colts, Jeb Witherspoon! I'll not ask you again."

Jeb dutifully handed his wife one of the colt revolvers. She tucked it in the sash of her riding skirt, a determined look on her face.

Jeb thought a minute. "Wait a minute," he said. "I just want to make sure it's fully loaded."

He retrieved the revolver and broke it down; it was loaded. Five shots could be fired before reloading. Just to be on the safe side he checked his as well. Then he pulled the colt rifle from its scabbard. It, too, was fully loaded – it could fire eight shots before reloading.

"Okay, Lottie, sweetheart. If we run into Jacks, make sure ever shot counts. We got eighteen chances to end this today. Now, one more thing I gotta do."

"And what's that, Jeb?"

"Raise your right hand, Lottie Witherspoon. By the power of the Republic of Texas, North Texas Division, I'm makin' you a Texas Ranger. Now, let's go get them bastards!"

Lottie smiled, but inside she was very much afraid. They spurred their horses the last three miles toward Stoney Canyon.

Chapter 36

Outside Brisbie, Texas
Saturday Afternoon
June 27, 1840

The Rangers came together after twenty minutes.

"Hell, they could have gone in any direction. It's almost useless." Harlan announced. "Too many tracks goin' in and out of town."

"I agree," Drummer joined in. "Usually I can spot strange or unusual stuff, but I'm stumped."

"Well," said Birdwell, let's bring all the boys back in. Where's Witherspoon? Is he back yet? Which direction did he head out to?"

Without waiting for an answer, George continued, "The Jacks' bunch probably didn't have time to split up the loot while they were here. They needed to join back up somewhere. Probably where

Jacks found those other four that joined him; Silver Creek. I say we go to Silver Creek."

"I don't think so, George," Drummer objected, "I checked for a mile and a half, for tracks headed to Silver Creek. The only tracks I saw were comin' into town."

Wilson answered Birdwell's mid-thought question, "Witherspoon ain't with us. He and Lottie headed out to Stoney Canyon to tell Tess the bad news."

Squire let out a whoop! "That's it, boys!" He yelled. "Marv Hightower's scratching in the blood. It wasn't a big X and a couple of squiggles. Marv was sending us a message. He was writing TESS! Jacks and his men are headed for the Hightower place in Stoney Canyon!"

Kentucky yelled, "Didn't I tell you Squire? Didn't I tell you? Yee Haw! Saddle up, boys! We gotta get to Stoney Canyon pronto. I told you, Squire. Didn't I?"

George yelled, "Dammit, Ranger! Stop giving orders!" But he smiled as he stepped up in his saddle.

Chapter 37

Stoney Canyon, Texas
Saturday Late Afternoon
June 27, 1840

Jacks and two companions sat their saddles in a little stand of Cottonwood trees, allowing their horses to graze on the tall grass while they gazed at the four large picture windows set in the sprawling stone structure in the clearing ahead. They were waiting for Blue.

"This must be the place boys. Quite a spread. Let's go introduce ourselves to Mr. Banker's widow, and offer our respects."

Another rider approached and joined them. Their little group was now complete.

Blue had been contemplating the meeting, and decided he would take a stand against Jacks.

"Jacks, we agreed to meet up here to split up the loot from the bank. I have a bad feelin' about stickin' around." Blue felt nervous and expressed it. "I'd as soon we sit right here under these trees and settle up. Then I'm off to parts unknown."

"Aw, come on, Blue... don't you want to at least meet the lady?"

"No, I don't. I just want the money an' I'm gone."

"But that's the thing, Blue. That house may just hold as much money as the bank did. We just may wind up so rich we don't ever have to do any more jobs."

Realizing that Jacks' argument, though not a strong one, was more persuasive, especially with the others in the group, Blue thought, *what the hell! Fifteen minutes won't hurt.*

"I ain't gonna draw on you, Jacks, but I'm disappointed. Sure, let's go meet the lady."

They crossed a swiftly flowing creek to approach the ranch house from the north, single file, avoiding the veranda which wrapped all around the front and most of the window-lined south side. The front door was a huge, solid slab of pecan, the window casings were of the same wood, set in the stone walls.

On the south veranda two upholstered rocking chairs were placed to overlook a sloping open green space which ended at the cottonwood–lined Stoney Creek.

~~~~~~~

Tess Hightower stood in the kitchen baking bread. Marv should have been home by now. He was only going in for the morning. Some business about the hotel.

She looked up to see movement along the
~~~~~~~

creek. Wiping her hands on her apron she reached for Marv's glass. Many times they had been thrilled at seeing a bear with cubs, a deer, a family of turkeys, or at times even three or four buffalo or a prowling cougar.

But today she saw something that didn't belong. She saw one, then two riders -- neither was familiar. She walked into her husband's private office and pulled two of his smooth-bore muskets from his gun rack. Then she changed her mind; she pulled an additional rifle from the rack, and a few extra shotgun shells.

She returned, arms loaded with weaponry, to the kitchen. Carefully and systematically, she lined the guns across the top of the long kitchen counter, then went back to a window for another close look across her lawn. Yet another rider had joined the first two at the creek.

"Marv Hightower, where are you?" Tess wasn't worried for herself. She lived in an almost impenetrable structure. She and Marv had held off an Apache raiding party three years ago. No, it was her husband she worried about. He should be here. Something very wrong had happened, and the reason was outside her door.

She pulled the bread from the oven – it was perfect. The kitchen took on the aroma of fresh bread. Normally, the aroma brought a sense of satisfaction... but not today.

She went back to the window. Four riders were crossing Stoney Creek and heading away from the house to the northeast.

"Ah," Tess spoke aloud to herself, "They're

heading around to the north to check it out; then they'll look at the roof and find that it's all Mexican tile. Then they'll take one last look at the front door and realize it can't be easily forced open, and then they'll come back to the south and try the windows. I won't drop the boards down, Marv. I'll leave them up, out of the way. That's where they'll make a try, But Tess will be waiting! I'll take care of them, Marv. I'll make them pay!"

She grabbed a bucket from the kitchen and made one last trip to her husband's office weapons rack. Choosing pouches of powder, wadding and balls, she dropped them in the bucket; the last piece of choice was her own pistol – a Colt repeating pistol her husband had bought for her on a lark when he was last down in Galveston for a meeting with Thomas McKinney and partners of the parent bank. It was fully loaded with five cartridges. It had never been fired.

Boots were jumping up and down, now, on the roof tiles, looking for weaknesses. The Apaches had tried that, too, she thought. These evil no-goods will crack a few, just like the Indian marauders did, but nothing Marv can't fi.... The thoughts of Marv being gone suddenly flooded her mind. She bit her lip. The next thing will be the front door, and then the windows. Tess Hightower was ready.

Chapter 38

Hightower Home
Stoney Canyon, Texas
Saturday Late Afternoon
June 27, 1840

The smoothbore blast sent flying glass into the sitting room and kitchen. Then a second blast with the same result. The shooter was not yet in sight. *Smart,* Tess thought. *Reload, you vile creature! It won't do you any good. Step through and you're still dead!*

Next came a small tumbleweed, fully engulfed in flame. *Fools! Floor is solid rock! I may lose that bearskin rug, but I never liked it anyway! And losing a nice chair or table would be horrible, but not as horrible as losing my life. Just be patient, Tess.*

At last, two crouching figures approached the window nearest the front corner of the Hightower fortress; one leg came through the shattered opening followed by a pistol and a torso. Upon seeing the torso, Tess pulled the trigger of one of the smoothbores; dropped it and reached for a second. The torso fell backward, pistol firing harmlessly in the kitchen's pecan ceiling.

Tess, now with the second shotgun, held her arms steady for the second man to make his try. Instead he retreated to a safe and secure distance, back around the corner. The wounded man wasn't making a sound or movement outside her window.

"How many cowards are outside?" Tess shouted. "Just the four of you or are there more? You willing to bet you can handle a helpless lady? I can't have any more weapons, can I? After all, my husband is a banker, not a gunslinger!"

The tumbleweed fire had gone out after the initial flare-up. She could see that the rooms were pretty much intact, and except for smoke that filled the upper two feet of the pitched ceiling, and the shattered glass which a broom would repair, all was in good shape.

She could hear some heated arguing going on outside, but couldn't ascertain the essence of the conversation. She prayed they would move on, leave her to deal with her emotions, her obvious losses, her future without Marv; to deal with being alone in Stoney Canyon, being alone ... in the great scheme of things.

Her prayer wasn't answered. Two ruffians rushed the two window openings simultaneously. She had already leveled her weapon in the center of one of the windows. It was now just a matter of pulling the trigger. Without emotion she squeezed, and watched one culprit, as if blown back through the window, to land four or five feet down the gentle slope. As she grabbed for the Colt revolver, the second villain was upon her, a knife in his hand, a garish grin on his face.

"I'll cut you to pieces, my little helpless lady," he snarled. His breath was hot and foul against her cheek; she was able to free her thumb from his lean stomach where he had it pinned, to draw back the hammer of the Colt.

The report of the gunshot was muffled, being so tightly jammed into the man's gut. He jumped back in surprised pain, then came at her again.

"You shot me! You're dead, you little Hussy!" he screamed. Her hand was now completely free. She pulled the hammer back and fired; again, and again, and again, and again. She continued to pull the hammer back and release it four or five times more, hearing only the sounds of ineffective clicks, before tremblingly dropping the colt to the floor, at the same time twisting herself away from her assailant.

Jacks fell over the counter, over her freshly baked bread, her assortment of readied weapons and ammunition, and finally came to rest with his head crashing against her kitchen stove, knocking the stovepipe loose and pouring soot down over his body.

Still shaking, Tess, as if in a trance, watched a fourth rider pull a saddlebag from a big grey horse across the way, toss it over the rump of a pretty Appaloosa, mount up, and trot slowly north right up the middle of Stoney Creek. She went back into the kitchen and grabbed the last long gun from the counter. Then she dragged the dead man out of her kitchen and set him on the lawn as far from her veranda as her strength allowed. The other two men quickly joined him.

Tess, now completely adrenalin drained, apron drenched in a mixture of blood and perspiration, sat in one of the two rocking chairs, head in hands, and stared at Stoney Creek as it meandered south, the long gun resting on her lap.

Jeb and Lottie found her there, rocking, sobbing, alone.

Chapter 39

Hightower Home
Stoney Canyon, Texas
Saturday Early Evening
June 27, 1840

George Birdwell and the detachment of Texas Rangers crossed Stoney Creek and joined Tess Hightower and the Witherspoons as dusk settled over the Stoney Canyon ranch. The kitchen was no longer soot-filled from the stove pipe catastrophe; the weapons had been reloaded and returned to the gun rack; the glass swept up and dropped to the bottom of the outhouse; the bread was tossed to the crows. Jeb reloaded Tess's Colt from his own supply of cartridges – adding a few extra cartridges to her supply as well; she elected to keep the Colt in her kitchen.

Squire and Lottie sat with Tess, while he went over the circumstances surrounding her husband's death; that it looked like he was struck with a heavy object and did not suffer. The bank was looted but nothing was found with the dead men, so perhaps the Jacks' band had stashed the valuables somewhere before riding out here.

Tess looked at Squire quizzically. "No one told you? There was a fourth rider. He pulled saddlebags off that big grey and put them on his Appaloosa and rode off going north, up the middle of the stream."

"Doesn't want anybody to track him. I'll have Drummer take a quick look along the banks to see if he can see where the rider left the stream."

"Well he can go for miles northwest. The creek is flat for a long way."

"Oh, I know, Ma'am. I know the area very well."

Birdwell walked over, concerned about the windows. "We need to put some boards on those openings. Mrs. Hightower, do you have any wood in the barn?"

Tess laughed, "Don't worry. Marv thought of everything. All four windows have pull-down wooden sheets that lock down for safety. We pull them down most evenings and raise them in the mornings."

Birdwell walked off the veranda. Looking at the three deceased, he shouted, "Fellas, let's get these three to Brisbie. We have a couple of people there who can identify who we have." Then, turning to Tess Hightower, he said, "Hopefully, one of these murderers is the leader, Maywell Jacks. We're mighty obliged to you one way or another, but he's not only a wanted man in the Texas Republic, but stateside as well. I'm not sure, but there may even be a cash reward out of Kansas for his capture or proof of his, uh, shall we say, dispatch to the other side."

"You mean 'shooting the scum and sending him straight to hell,' Ranger. Am I right?"

"Yes, Ma'am."

"I'd be happy to receive any reward on behalf of the losses the bank suffered."

"That's mighty kind, Ma'am."

"Please. Tess!"

"That's mighty kind, Tess."

Lottie finished cleaning in the kitchen. It would pass Tess's inspection, she thought. She walked outside to the south veranda, emptied the wash water from a bucket, wrung the excess water from the towel she'd been using, and set the bucket upside down. Then she spread the towel on the bucket to dry, and walked over to join Squire and the widow.

"I think we should saddle up a horse for you, and bring you into Brisbie for a day or so, Tess. You need time to sort things out, and you need friends around you, to make use of, as often or as little as you need."

"Oh, Lottie, thanks for the suggestion," Tess sighed. "I've been sitting here feeling sorry for myself, and wondering how I could ask the fellows if I could tag along. I need to make arrangements, I need the proper clothing, I need to make some important assessments regarding my future with the bank and the good folks of Brisbie."

"I'll have your horse saddled right away, Mrs. Hightower," Squire promised. "That's a pinto if I'm not mistaken."

"Yes, the pinto."

As Jeb Witherspoon walked by, he overheard the conversation, and tipped his hat to Squire, indicating he would fetch the pinto.

"Not much gets past you does it, Ranger?" continued Tess, "except, I just told George Birdwell to call me Tess. No reason for you to be so formal at this stage," she chided.

"I appreciate your permission, but forgive me if I forget a time or two. I was reared to treat ladies with a certain amount of respect whether they be twenty or one hundred twenty," Squire grinned and touched his hat brim. Then he added soberly, "Especially, Ma'am, at a time like this, I prefer the formality."

Tess fumbled for a proper response. "Perfectly understood," she said.

The Rangers announced the dead had been roped to horses and they were ready to ride.

Lottie leaned over and wrapped her arm around Tess Hightower. "Your pony is here, Tess. Let's get you to Brisbie."

Chapter 40

Brisbie, Texas
Saturday Early Evening
June 27, 1840

An Appaloosa trotted down Main Street and pulled up in front of the sheriff's office. No one in town even noticed.

The young rider threw his leg over the saddle and dismounted, tossed his reins over the hitching post, pulled the saddlebags off the neck of the pony, casually opened the door and walked inside.

"Howdy, boys," he greeted those in the cell, smiling at Chester Smitts and Buddy, and casting a sneering nod of recognition at Crazy Red.

"Blue! Yore a sight fer sore eyes! You gonna spring us? We're gonna end up on a rope if'n you don't," Buddy blurted out.

"Haven't got time. Sorry, Buddy. Just here for a little business, an' then I'm gone," he said, emptying the saddlebags on the desk. "Wheeeeoo!" Blue whistled, as badges and money fell from the bags. "Jacks had a serious hate for lawmen!" He counted twenty-two badges including some from Kansas and Missouri.

"Where is Jacks?" Buddy asked. "Is he with you? An' the others?"

"Naw. I came on ahead. I expect they'll be along shortly."

"Where you off to, Blue?" Smitty asked. "Californey? I bet its Californey, ain't it?"

"Could be. Haven't rightly decided yet, but not Galveston. That's fer damn shore!"

He grabbed the empty saddlebags, reached for three more U.S. coins on the sheriff's desk, "Just to make sure I have enough," he winked.

"You got our loot!" Crazy Red howled. "Boys he got Brisbie's loot an' looks like he's givin' it back!"

"No, Red, I'm takin' *my share* of the loot. That's all!" Blue responded, laughing.

He slung the saddlebags over a shoulder and pocketed the coins. "These are just a few extra to go with what I already have in my own saddlebags!"

He tipped his hat, opened the door, and walked out, shutting the door firmly behind him.

The three inside were screaming expletives at him as he mounted the spotted pony and trotted out of Brisbie. No one in town even noticed.

Chapter 41

Brisbie, Texas
Saturday Evening
June 27, 1840

The tired troop of Rangers with the ladies and the three horses carrying their burdens reached Brisbie much later in the evening.

Lottie took Tess directly to the *Good Night* Hotel, where they were greeted by Suzanna Knight.

"We might just fill up the hotel tonight, Suzanna," Lottie announced. "Good news, though. Jacks is dead, we think. Wilson, er, Sheriff Tanner is taking Buddy over to identify the three dead killers. Tess, here, shot them all!"

"Oh, Tess!" Suzanna exclaimed. "Are you okay? Oh, you poor dear!" Suzanna began to fuss over the widow Hightower; had her sit down with a cup of tea and a warm scone.

"Suzanna, stop!" Tess laughed. "I'm fine, now! But, for a time it seemed I was almost in a coma.

Those awful men! They were trying to come through my windows; there was blood everywhere, and my freshly baked bread was ruined, and one of them just about destroyed my stove-- or at least the stovepipe-- soot over everything! And the worst part is that Marv is gone. Marv is gone!"

Tess burst out crying; then she burst out in a fit of laughter mixed with choking, which lasted more than a minute. Finally she was back in control.

"Oh, that was good! I feel so much better! Sorry for my outburst, but I guess I needed that!"

Lottie put her arms around her, Suzanna did the same, and the three of them stood in a circle trying to relax and recover from the extreme range of emotions each had dealt with over the last forty-eight hours.

~~~~~~~~

Squire, Witherspoon and Drummer took the bodies down from the horses and dragged them to the Mortician's workshop. They pounded on his door, but no one was around.

"Kentucky, go round up Sanders, tell him we need to throw some more work on 'im," Wilson said. "I'll run over and get Buddy to identify them; make sure we know we got the right bunch."

Drummer took the horses' reins and said, "I know, I know, *'Drummer, take these nags over to the stables and water'em an' feed'em.'* I don't mind though. At least they're better company than the ones I ride *with* most times."

About that time the sheriff's door opened across the way.

"Men, you ain't gonna believe this!" Wilson whooped, as he dragged Buddy down the steps of
~~~~~~~~

the sheriff's office. "Buddy here says our bank's money, leastwise most of it, got returned this evening by that Blue fella. He musta been the fourth outlaw out at Hightower's."

"Well, I'll be!" whistled Witherspoon. "Now ain't thet sumthin!"

George Birdwell was just joining the group. Buddy looked at the three men sprawled out in front of Sanders Mortuary, shaking his head. "Guess Blue was right, said they'd be along shortly. Didn't say they'd be strung over the backs of ponies."

Milton Sanders came along about that time, still hanging onto his overalls, trying to keep up with Kentucky while buckling one of his shoulder straps on. He reached his workshop in time to hear Buddy: "This one here is Chino -- he's the one that rides a good lookin' Appaloosa, an' this one here is Isaiah, last name is Bennett or Bernard. Stutters a lot, well he did stutter a lot, and this one," Buddy paused, "this one is my cousin, Maywell Jacks."

George Birdwell blew out a long breath. "So we finally got him!" Turning to Witherspoon, he asked, "What was that cousin of his saying about Blue being right?"

"Seems the fourth member of the gang that went out to the Hightower's spread left with a saddlebag full of the bank's money, and dropped it off at the sheriff's office," Witherspoon replied. "Not only thet, but they was more'n twenty silver badges in his bags."

"What?" George raged. "How many?" he asked incredulously.

"Twenty-two to be exact," Buddy spoke up. "I guess I'se responsible for one or two, but I never thought he had that menny. I'm shore sorry. I shudda left Jacks years ago."

George just glared at Buddy. "Get him back to his cell!" he thundered to Wilson.

"Well, if that don't beat all!" George whistled, shaking his head.

~~~

"I'm going over to ask how many are stayin' the night," Lottie informed the two other ladies. "They'll probably want something to eat and also something for breakfast tomorrow morning."

"Alice will help out with breakfast," Suzanna yelled out as Lottie walked out the door.

The evening breeze felt good! The ordeal was finally over. Lottie felt a ton of stressful anxiety flow from her neck and shoulders.

All she wanted now was to curl up with Jeb and talk foolishness about retiring, about lazing on a trout stream with her toes dangling in the cold, swift, splashing blue water -- ignoring the trout nibbling on her line as she and Jeb nibble on each other; or maybe a picnic basket with a checkered tablecloth, on the banks of that trout stream; or maybe simply enjoying each other, skinny dipping *in* that trout stream. *Oh, Jacob Witherspoon,* she shook her head back and forth. *We are so blessed!*

Lottie came back to reality as she approached a group of Rangers discussing the return of the bank's money. She asked the question she had come to ask. The answer was nine. She told them the meal and rooms would be ready in half an hour. Then she walked slowly back to the *Good Night,* picking up her daydream where she had left off -- in the middle of a trout stream.
~~~

Chapter 42

Brisbie, Texas
Sunday
June 28, 1840

Sunday morning Pastor Jenkins preached a fine sermon about the resurrection and hellfire; very appropriate as over in the Sanders workshop there were five caskets filled with five of Brisbie's upstanding, and five filled with outlaws who needed nothing more than to await their fate. The sermon spoke to both those groups, and to any listening who might be sitting on the fence.

To a thunderous applause it was announced that most of the bank's money had been miraculously recovered. A bass voice started singing _Bringing In The Sheaves_ and the whole assembly joined in. It was, overall, a joyous service.

Birdwell and his two Rangers left for home Sunday afternoon. George promised to find an able-bodied bookkeeper-type for the Brisbie Bank, and would also find out if there was a monetary reward for the dispatching of Maywell Jacks. He also promised to have every Ranger in his division equipped with the Colt weapons. Before leaving, he had a final gathering with the Rangers about a rumor he had heard just before coming back to Brisbie.

"Seems the Indian Tribes are having a big pow-wow southeast of here, down around Franklin - - Brazos River territory. I think ol' Lamar has stirred them all up: Shoshone, Apache, Comanche, Kiowa, Pawnee, and more. I'm telling you this for obvious reasons; we may have an Indian war on our hands." Birdwell made a distasteful face, shook his head, and continued, "I, for one, would rather we have a bit more harmony. I'd stay out of Indian Territory if you can."
George finished by saying, "Men, I'm proud of what we've done here. That includes Tess Hightower. Texas is grateful."

Squire pulled Birdwell aside. "George, that fella they call Crazy Red had a packed money belt on him. I'm going to split it up with the boys. There will be enough for Tess if there's no reward money for her."

"Suit yourself Daniels. God knows we don't get half of what we're worth. Take care."

<center>~~~~~~~</center>

Brisbie, Texas
Monday
June 29, 1840

Monday morning Harlan Franklin stopped by the sheriff's office on his way out of town.

"Wilson," he said, shaking the young lawman's

hand, "you have a big job here in Brisbie, but I think you'll fill Tom's boots very nicely. I don't ride with too many fellas, but I'd ride with you again, and call you friend."

"Thank you Harlan, an' that goes fer me as well."

"Oh, wait! Damn! I almost fergot!" Franklin reached into his vest pocket and pulled out a small key attached to a string.

"I think you'll find this key fits a drawer in the back of the safe in the bank. Marv had, like a false back to the val'ables box. You gotta pull the back out, an' you'll find a bunch of locked drawers. Under them you'll see a bigger drawer. This key fits that bigger drawer, I'm sure of it. An' I bet all the other keys are in that drawer! Mebbe all the folks' val'ables

"How'd you get it?"

"It was on Marv when he died. I been thinkin' on it for a day or two, and I think I got it right. If it don't, then I don't know what it might be fer."

Then, shaking hands again, "So long, Wilson."

"Have a safe journey, Harlan."

~~~~~~~

Milton Sanders was a busy man. So busy, he in fact, hired two townsfolk to dig some graves. There was a small plot for the general public. The surveyor and the young Indian were delegated to that plot; Sheriff Tom Lewis, a single man, was

given a spot on a knoll under a Red Oak tree; Suzanna's father, Frank Knight had a family plot with an iron fence around it. He'd always hoped he would live to see his grandchildren before he went
~~~~~~~

to rest there, but that was not to be; the banker, Marv Hightower hadn't chosen a plot, but Tess asked that he be buried in a grassy area near some Texas Redbud trees where from time to time deer had been seen grazing.

As far as the outlaws were concerned, Milton decided they would go in a row along a far wall. He had his crew dig three extras for the three in jail; he would build their caskets on the morrow; a separate crew was already building the gallows today – Monday. Sheriff Wilson Tanner said the hanging would be Wednesday, July one.

Milton frowned. *Counting those three in jail,* he mused, *that's thirteen burials all within a short time.* "That's not a good omen," Milton said aloud to nobody in particular, "but then, thirteen times eleven dollars is the best payout I ever had."

"I'll have to pay six dollars and fifty cents for the grave digging, and an average of one dollar and fifty cents for the wood from the sawyer, Jefferson out west on the outskirts of town, to make the boxes. That's another nineteen dollars and fifty cents. That leaves me with -- Wow! That leaves me with one hundred and seventeen dollars!"

After instructing the diggers where to dig, Milton got in his buggy and drove back to his workshop; he grabbed his hammer and nails and continued putting together the next casket.

<p style="text-align:center">~~~~~~~</p>

Jefferson's wagon drove to the center of town, where a crew of six men waited to offload the necessary lumber. Wilson watched the progress. He knew that as sheriff, he should be directing the building and erecting of the hanging platform, but he was a newcomer to this necessary part of his job so he left it to the more experienced Witherspoon, and simply took notes. Besides, there were twelve to fifteen other *experts* standing around, telling the builders *how it should be done.*

Witherspoon wouldn't allow the ropes to go up until early Wednesday morning. That way, no boisterous or unruly children, (or husbands, Jeb joked) could get strangled by accidently getting themselves entangled in the nooses.

~~~~~~~~

Wilson walked over to the *Good Night Hotel* to ask Tess Hightower to accompany him to the bank. Along the way, they picked up Drummer and Squire.

"Harlan gave me a key before he left, Ma'am. He said there's a secret compartment in the back of the strong box in your husband's office. I think we should all take a look, so there's no question or quarrel about the contents. Hopefully, this key will unlock a drawer in the 'vault'."

They all entered the little chamber. It had been washed clean of Navarro's blood, and all traces of disturbance gone. Wilson knelt down and opened the strong box.

"I don't see nothin', Squire, do you?"

Squire joined him on the floor. "Yes. See that little hole, way in the back wall? Reach in and see if you can pull the whole wall out using your finger through that hole."

Wilson reached in, stuck his finger through and gave it a jerk. The wall popped out, revealing
~~~~~~~~

the drawers just as Harlan had said.

"Well, I'll be dogged!"

Taking the key, he tried the bottom drawer. It clicked. He pulled it open to reveal several papers and upwards of thirty keys, each one stamped with a number matching the numbers on the drawers above the bottom one. He handed the papers to Tess, who looked at the two columns across the top and read: "Number one. Next to it is the name Harold Mansfred. Oh! I see," she exclaimed! "That box number one belongs to Harold Mansfred, and so on. Harold must have all his important papers in that box. How clever! It's like a little vault in what should be the safest place in town!"

"Okay, I've seen enough," Wilson decided for them all. "We don't need to snoop any further. I think we can tell the folks that if they have any personal things of value in the bank, it's all safe, don't you?"

They all agreed. They put things back as they had found them. Wilson put the key in his pocket.

They walked back into the street. The "hanging platform" was complete. Townsfolk were gathered round it, discussing the pros and cons of hanging as a remedy for such a heinous crime, but the consensus was that public hanging was the *only* remedy, because it put the fear into all observers, and contemplators of crime.

Chapter 43

Brisbie, Texas
Tuesday
June 30, 1840

News of the upcoming hanging spread throughout the whole of northeast Texas. People began showing up in droves to witness the spectacle. By afternoon, Main Street in Brisbie was a beehive of activity.

Every saloon was bulging with too many heavy drinkers, every hotel -- from *The Good Night* to *The Texas Star* -- was completely booked to overflowing; even a few rooms were shared by total strangers desperate to simply find a place to lay their heads for the night.

Every eating establishment was forced to, at times, borrow a certain ingredient from another to prepare an entree for a patron. Business was good! But the carnival atmosphere was worrying to Sheriff Wilson Tanner. Any crowd was worrying, but a rowdy, drunken crowd could easily get out of hand.

The lawman was happy that four Rangers were still in town. One problem he hoped could be avoided: having to arrest a drunk. Where would he put him?

That possibility came sooner than Wilson wanted to find out. Gunshots came from *The Wounded Buffalo.* Patrons tumbled out the doors and into the street. Kentucky, who was closer, entered the establishment a few moments before Wilson.

"Who fired that shot?" the old Ranger yelled above the noisy, laughing, screaming din. "What's goin' on in here?" he yelled again. This time he got the attention of the patrons.

"Hey, Kentucky! Monty an' I was just showin' Jonathan that trick you showed us. You know, how we shoot the center out of the ace of spades? I'm about ready to take my turn. Monty was scared to stick the ace on my hatband, so we stuck it on top of a whiskey glass. Look here! He hit it plumb center! Didn't spill a drop!"

"Dan! Not tonight, Dan. I ain't a gonna take yore guns, but I don't wanna hear no more gunshots! We'd have to add one more noose fer tomorrow if sumthin' turrible was to happen."

Wilson heard the conversation. "What? Kentucky! Shooting aces off a hatband in a saloon?"

"Well, it was a long time ago, Sheriff. And it was fun at the time."

"Uh-huh, what's a long time ago, Kentucky?"

"A week or so at least, Sheriff." Kentucky gave Wilson a sidelong grin.

"Yeah, that's what I thought."

The rest of the day, surprisingly, was without incident. The sheriff and four Rangers mingled with the crowds; just their presence was central to keeping the peace.

The prisoners in the jail cell were of course well aware of their circumstances. At 6 p.m. Wilson and Squire walked into the jail.

"You fellas will be hanged tomorrow mornin' at 10 a.m., for the atrocities committed against the Republic of Texas. I'm goin' over to *The Copperhead* with your 'last meal' requests. I'm also bringin' a bottle to the jail. So fellas, what'll it be?"

All three sat, sober and silent. Finally Chester Smitts said, "Squire, I guess I'll have a nice big steak. An' maybe some corn on the cob if they got any."

The other two chimed in and agreed that was a good choice. "If they ain't got corn, I'll take some baked beans," said Buddy. "That's always a good choice."

"Yeah."

Chapter 44

Brisbie, Texas
8:30 Wednesday Morning
July 1, 1840

Wednesday morning dawned warm and muggy. The prisoners received a breakfast from *The Good Night Hotel* – ironically, it consisted of the same fare they had received the previous Friday morning -- flapjacks, scrambled eggs and thick cuts of side bacon, washed down with strong, black coffee.

Dozens of gawkers were already milling around the platform, even though it was only 8:30 a.m. Witherspoon suggested they string up some ropes to keep a zone between the platform and the spectators. That suggestion was quickly agreed to and implemented by some of the work crew.

Pastor Jenkins sat on one end of the platform, bible in his lap, flipping from one passage to another, placing slips of paper in certain places, and writing notes in a writing pad of sorts.

An empty chair was set on the platform next to the pastor, awaiting the hangman. Next to the hangman's chair was a three-foot plank of lumber standing vertically. Pastor Jenkins had brought both chairs up, Witherspoon decided. Looking at that ominous chair made chills run up and down his spine. He'd seen a few hangings in his time; they always seemed so formal, so stark, so final.

In the center of the platform was an eight-foot long trapdoor in the floor; above the trapdoor the gallows-tree, outfitted just this morning with three knotted nooses for the three villains. All was ready. The crowds began to gather.

Brisbie, Texas
9:20 Wednesday Morning
July 1, 1840

Wilson looked at the clock on his wall - 9:20 a.m. His prisoners kept looking at the same clock. No words were spoken. Each of them sat in a different corner, alone.

Outside, near the center of attraction, Kentucky and Drummer decided to walk through the crowd, while Witherspoon took his place along the rope barrier. Squire walked up and down Main Street just to avert any foolish ideas outsiders might consider during the hanging.

Suddenly a woman screamed. Shots were fired and the crowd began to disperse. More screams were heard as people ran from the street into the sheltering hotel and saloons.

Squire came running from in front of the blacksmith shop. Kentucky pulled his colt and looked in every direction to spot the cause of the disturbance. Drummer and Witherspoon saw the cause, but Witherspoon was the first to react.

"Hold yer fire! Everbody! No shootin'!" He could be heard above the shouting and screaming of the crowd.

No one was paying attention to the gallows! Instead, they were looking up the north end of Main Street just beyond the edge of Brisbie.

Kentucky and Drummer joined Witherspoon as they stood and stared at a band of Kiowa horsemen, at least eight, maybe ten, who sat as statues observing the scene before them.

"Kentucky, put yore gun away. Drummer, come with me." Witherspoon started walking, casually, steadily up the street. Drummer, a little less sure, walked at his side.

Squire Daniels, by this time, was standing on the platform along with Pastor Jenkins for a better view of the proceedings at the end of town.

As the two Rangers got near, two Kiowa braves urged their horses forward, slid down from their ponies and offered a wave of the arm in greeting. Witherspoon and Drummer did the same.

The four were joined in conversation for some minutes, both in sign and with Witherspoon's understanding of a smattering of Comanche, Kiowa and Pawnee; the Indians seemed impressed.

Drummer came trotting back to the platform. "They want to speak with you, Squire. Seems they know you."

"They know me? I don't think....unless, Ahhh, I know. It's my blood brother, isn't it? He's one of them."

Squire, unlike the other Rangers, pulled his

colt rifle from the scabbard as he passed by his pony, and walked with Drummer, rifle slung over his shoulder. As they reached the Kiowa, he offered a greeting as he had seen demonstrated earlier, and smiled a warm smile at his new, red brother -- one of the two lead braves.

"Squire, this brave is anxious to greet you formally. His name is *Apiatan*. It means 'Wooden Lance'. I told him your name is Squire an' that it means 'Wise One'. I hope you don't mind, but these redskins are pretty much set on the meanin' of names, an' it was the first thing thet popped into my head. When you greet him, just hold your hand out, palm up."

"That's just fine, Jeb. So I suppose your name means 'Dried-up Gourd'?" Squire laughed.

"Sumthin like thet," Witherspoon said, wryly.

"An' I played up Drummer here, as well. He's now 'Moon Tracker'. He can track even at night if need be." Then turning to the young Ranger, Jeb said, "Drummer, you stay out of any conversation for the time bein'. They're here on business. Not sure yet what kind, but to be sure, they have somethin' to discuss."

"Okay, but did you really tell them that about me?" Drummer asked.

"Why, shore! They respect that kind o' talk." Squire approached the young brave. "Friend!" he said. *"Apiatan -- friend!"* He held out his hand palm up. Immediately *Apiatan* took it in his own and held it firmly for so long, Squire wondered if he would never let go. The brave repeated "Ski-yer. Friend. Sky-yir. Friend."

"This here is *Kgyi-yo* which means 'Grizzly Bear'/', so I'm guessin' he either fought one or killed one, or his Ma saw one while he was still in the womb," Witherspoon said, in identifying the second brave.

Squire held his hand out as before, but Grizzly Bear simply nodded and said, "Ski-yer", and nodded again.

"*Kgyi-yo*", Squire gave it his best try, and came close to the correct pronunciation. A slight smile curled the corners of Grizzly Bear's mouth. He grunted approvingly.

A short period of silence followed. The residents and visitors of Brisbie brave enough to venture forth, waited to see how the Kiowa visit would play out; men held their weapons at the ready, women, now more curious than frightened, watched every motion of the five men. Witherspoon finally asked the reason for the visit.

Grizzly Bear looked at the little group of Kiowa behind him and beckoned with his arm. An older warrior with full headdress walked his horse forward. Grizzly Bear introduced him to the Rangers as Chief **Teh-too-tsa**, elder chief of the **Kiowa nation.**

The elder chief spoke at length with Witherspoon, thanking Squire for mending and caring for his wounded warrior *Apatian,* and for treating the dead warriors with dignity, even positioning their bodies ceremoniously.

Further, he thanked them for staying out of Indian Territory except as required, but would they please eliminate building more settlements in the fringe areas, would they please stop the buffalo hunters from senseless slaughter, seeking only buffalo hides. He promised in return that the Kiowa

would influence their cousins, the Comanche to leave Brisbie and the surrounding areas from any raiding parties; that the two populations could live in peace.

By now it was after 10 a.m. The prisoners sat in the cell wondering why their fate had not come to the expected climax. They had heard the commotion outside but when Wilson went out they were left without explanation.

Back outside the meeting continued. Squire was saying he would try his best to have buffalo hunters outlawed from the north Texas plains, but it's like the Crow or Blackfoot coming down to Kiowa land and stealing horses – hard to control.

"Um!" said Teh-too-tsa. He understood.

Now came the crux of the visit.

The old Chief said, "'*Rojo encabezados por el hombre medicina loca*'! We understand you have him as a prisoner. We want him to be released to us!"

Witherspoon translated for the Rangers. The three looked at each other in amazement. After a short discussion, Witherspoon turned to Chief Teh-too-tsa.

"Chief, Squire says we have our laws that we must follow. Do you see the wooden structure we erected in town?" he said, pointing. "We just built that structure. We have three men in a prisoner compound. Just this mornin' they are goin' to be punished – hanged until they die for crimes against our people, crimes of murder, stealin' and torturin'. This '*Rojo encabezados por el hombre medicina loca*' is one of them. We call him 'Crazy Red'. We will punish him this mornin'!"

Now it was the Old Chief's turn to look at his comrades, questioning. After some discussion he turned to the lawmen.

"Is 'Blood Woman' here?" he asked. "She's *'Rojo encabezados por el hombre medicina loca's* squaw."

Again the three Rangers looked at each other questioning. Squire finally said, "I have an idea. Tell the chief that Brisbie would consider it an honor if the chief and all of his braves sit on the platform to observe the hanging."

Chief Teh-too-tsa said, after consulting once more with his advisors, "We will do this thing! We will sit on the platform to watch you deal out justice the way of the white man. You will sit beside me, Ski-yir at my left arm."

"Ah," said Squire to Witherspoon, "and what brave will be at his right...or will it be you, Witherspoon?"

"And Blood Woman will be at my right," the chief continued, to the grunts of approval from his warriors. It was final.

As the Kiowa walked their horses back to the larger group, the three Rangers trotted back to the platform on Main Street. Looking back, Squire wondered what they were in for. All ten warriors were walking their ponies toward town, led by Chief Teh-too-tsa sitting stately astride his beautiful pinto.

Chapter 45

Brisbie, Texas
10:50 Wednesday Morning
July 1, 1840

Three pews from the church were brought to the platform and placed on one end for the native dignitaries. Then three comfortable chairs were set in front of the pews.

Some of the out-of-towners had gone long before 10 a.m. for fear of the Kiowa; left now were mostly locals.

"Kentucky, fetch Miss Suzanna from the hotel. Tell her to remain calm and come see Squire. Then once that's done, tell Wilson to bring the prisoners at 11 a.m."

Suzanna appeared next to Squire. "Isn't that the Indian you bandaged up?" pointing at Apiatan.

"Yes it is, Blood Woman," Squire smiled.

"You didn't! Squire Daniels! No! No!"

"Shush! Suzanna, you must understand. This is the Chief of the Kiowa. He is attending the hanging as a guest. He wants the Blood Woman sitting beside him."

"What? That's even worse! I hadn't planned on attending the hanging, and now you've made me a part of it?"

Wilson was pushing the shackled prisoners to the platform. Witherspoon ushered the warriors to the pews at the end. Pastor Jenkins who had left when the Kiowa came, returned to his place.

Squire looked at Suzanna. "The chief will follow me. You follow the chief and sit on his right." Squire then mounted the steps, Chief Teh-too-tsa on his heels.

Suzanna was angry! Very angry! She stormed up the steps, glared at Squire as she passed him, and even frowned at the elder Kiowa as she seated herself at his right hand.

Thinking to herself that she had acted as a spoiled brat, she turned to him with as cordial a quick smile as she could muster, then sat stiffly. The chief looked her up and down, pursed his lips and nodded approvingly. Then he, too, sat stiffly, following her example.

Last to reach the gallows before the prisoners was Jefferson, the hangman.

The three outlaws were led up, hands tied behind their back and shackled in leg-irons. They now stood over the trapdoor. Crazy Red was still wearing that, by now, dingy top hat. He looked at the Kiowa chief, then at the entourage at the platform's end, and finally at Suzanna. "Good morning, Blood Woman," he laughed. She ignored him. Chief Teh-too-tsa approved.

The hangman stood, slipped a noose around the neck of each prisoner and drew each rope rather tight. He removed Crazy Red's top hat, and set it on the floor behind the trapdoor. Then he retired to his chair.

Pastor Jenkins was noticeably unnerved by the Kiowa; he forgot any preparation he may have had, and simply asked the three if they had any last words.

Buddy had some words of remorse, "I bin thinkin' all these years, it weren't no Rangers kilt Maywell's folks. It were redskins that done it." He looked over at the Kiowa, thankful they didn't understand. "If I'd only split up with Jacks when I was twenty I'd maybe be a bank clerk by now, or a lawman. I'm sorry I kilt some good men."

Chester Smitts rambled on and on, "I was dead last week. I knew it then. I should have stayed in Kansas. I knew it, but I can't blame Lulu. I can only blame myself. Me an' Buddy here, are like two old friends who just keep drinking and find ourselves drunk and so, we go walkin' arm in arm, fallin' in the mud. Each time we got up, we find ourselves dirtier an' dirtier. God forgive me."

Crazy Red again looked over at the guests. No look of remorse at all on his face. "Another thirty years would have been fun. I'd tip my hat to the ladies but my hands are in shackles -- oh, yeah, an' I ain't got no hat."

Suzanna spat at him, "Today justice is served, you filth!"

"Hold yer tongue! This is my time, Blood Woman!" he responded loudly.

The Kiowa chief didn't flinch during this exchange. And then, Crazy Red turned to the Kiowa. And in their tongue said, "You are my people. I beg your mercy, not these whites who are your enemies, and mine. They will try to take our land and our resources; they are greedy, they increase like grasshoppers!"

Chief Teh-too-tsa spat at him exactly as Suzanna had. Then he spoke harshly in the Kiowa tongue, "Today justice is served, you filth!"

The Kiowa entourage murmured grunts of approval at their chief's remark; Suzanna feeling the tone of his severity, remained as stoic as the situation allowed, but a glimmer of satisfaction crossed her face.

Witherspoon sucked in a large breath of air in surprise. "That sly old Fox," he whispered to Drummer. "He understands the language. I'll bet he speaks it, too."

Crazy Red continued in English, "I guess I won't get those thirty years. Hee hee! It's been fun! By the way, Chief Teh-too-tsa, there, why he's sizing up your town, to see your manpower; your strength. That way, he can determine how many scalps he'll take when he rides in here with his war paint on. Too bad I won't be around to see that! Hee heee! Oh well, do what you came to do."

The crowds that had gathered earlier had all but disappeared. Only a few die-hard out-of-towners along with a handful of locals remained to hear Pastor Jenkins or to watch the hanging itself.

"May God have mercy on your souls," is all Pastor Jenkins said.

Wilson indicated to Jefferson that it was time. Jefferson stood, pushed the vertical wooden lever next to his chair, releasing the trap door. The three men dropped through the floor. Just that quick. It was over.

A startled Chief Teh-too-tsa stood, walked to the gaping hole, looked down at the three lifeless bodies, showed a slight grimace on his face, then grunted an approving, "Ummm." His entire troupe followed his example.

On his way off the platform, *Kgyi-yo* picked up the top hat, wiped it free of dust, and put it on his head.

When Squire came down from the gallows Witherspoon took him aside. "Chief knows Yankee, Squire. Mind how you talk."

Daniels understood. "Maybe Blood Woman would like to have that information," he suggested nodding to the young lady, who was by now surrounded by their special guests.

Both Rangers sidled up to Suzanna and shielded her from the braves who were curious and intrigued to see Blood Woman.

Squire suggested that she bring out a pitcher of water and some cups or glasses, which she was quick to do. The Kiowa stood in front of the hotel for ten minutes or more, drinking water and discussing the strange ways of the white man.

Then, abruptly the chief motioned that they should leave. He came up to the Rangers, and held his hand out for Squire to take. Daniels took it and held it for a full two seconds, then released it.

"Thank you for being in attendance," he told the chief. "As you have seen, we deal with criminals in a swift and decisive way."

Almost the whole town of Brisbie reappeared, and stood on Main Street. They watched until the band of Kiowa was out of sight. Then almost the whole town of Brisbie let out one very big sigh of relief.

Witherspoon finally turned on his heel, "It's been one helluva day," he said to no one in particular.

~~~~~~~~

It was a week for rejoicing. The Jacks' bunch had been dismantled, Jacks was gone. Crazy Red and the other two prisoners in the jail would no longer be a problem, and the Kiowa Chief had become a neighbor of sorts. At least, he and his band was now a known entity, not a violent unknown.
~~~~~~~~

Chapter 46

Brisbie, Texas
Regarding the Bank
Wednesday Morning
July 8, 1840

George Birdwell, true to his word, had an experienced banker sent to Brisbie to assist Jimmy Mann. The fella was a middle aged, bearded gent, named Trevor Hardaway.

After meeting with Jimmy Mann and the town's leaders, Hardaway went to work. He went through all the ledgers and other bank documents, found almost everything he was looking for but not everything.

"It looks like that fella, Blue, ended up with just shy of $600.00," he said, which agreed exactly with Mann's figures. "Now, how did you pay the mortician for the work he did?"

"The town picked that up. We passed the hat and all pitched in," replied Jimmy.

"Okay. Won't change that now. How are you paying the sheriff? Payday is the first of the month;

has he got paid yet? And how about the Rangers? Where is the ledger for their pay? And the credit against their land claims?'

Jimmy Mann was at a loss with Hardaway's no-nonsense approach. He threw his arms up and said, "Let me go get Tanner. Seems I remember he has something belongs to the bank."

"Yeah, I got a key. C'mon. I'll show you." The young sheriff responded. Wilson accompanied Jimmy to the bank. They found the hidden cabinet together, and the key opened the bottom drawer. From there, Hardaway took over. It took a week, but by the time Hardaway left, Jimmy Mann was well in control of the Brisbie branch of the Thomas McKinney Bank of Galveston.

Chapter 47

Brisbie, Texas
Regarding the Hotel
Wednesday Morning
July 8, 1840

Suzanna had no trouble managing the hotel. Kitchen help and maid service was easier than she had anticipated; several townsfolk came forth to apply. Only a part of her working capital had been returned from the Jacks' robbery, but she thought possibly she could get a loan from the bank.

Hardaway was still there when Suzanna went to the bank. When she requested a loan, Hardaway informed her that she already had a loan, which was coming due in November.

"Let me check something," said Hardaway. He pored over some papers and finally said, "Aha!"

"Your father has a box safe in the back, Suzanna. I remembered seeing his name on these papers. Jimmy, grab the box and the key for Miss Suzanna. Jimmy Manns went to the back, opened the bottom drawer, plucked out key #14 and brought out box #14. Suzanna opened it.

Inside were papers and some cash – both paper and gold coins. She read the first paper carefully. It was a bank loan, not against the hotel, but against a four thousand acre piece of land south of Brisbie. Owing on it was a balance of $1,100.00.

She read the second paper. It was his last will and testament bequeathing everything to her. It had been witnessed by a few citizens in Galvaston. It was entirely legal.

She began counting the money, tears in her eyes. When she got to $4,000.00, she stopped counting, although there was much more. Miss Knight burst into tears.

She pulled herself together, and turned to the banker. "Here, Jimmy. $1,100.00. My goodness! Sign that property over to me! Right this minute, Jimmy, before I faint!"

She pocketed another $1,000, pushed the box across the table toward Jimmy, and said "Put the box back, please." Then she stepped, excitedly, out of the bank.

"Yes, Ma'am," he called after her.

~~~~~~~

When Banker Hardaway rode into town, he had delivered news to Squire that there had been Comanche raids down along the Trinity River, and that all available Rangers were needed to ride southeast as soon as possible. Squire received the news solemnly, and mulled it over for a few days before acting on it. Finally he called the other three into the hotel dining room for breakfast. He asked Jeb to bring Lottie in, even though the Witherspoons
~~~~~~~

lived twelve miles out of town on the Little Red River.

"Well gents, seems the Comanche are raising a ruckus down on the Trinity, and ol' George wants a few of us down there. Get your gear prepared; we'll ride out tomorrow morning."

"Jeb," Squire continued, taking a sidelong look at Lottie, "I'm leaving you here. Wilson will need some help for a couple of months, and Lottie needs you right now."

Witherspoon started to complain, but Lottie looked up at him with pleading eyes, so he stopped, looked down at her and put his arms around her.

"Alright, Lottie," he said.

Brisbie, Texas
Saying Goodbye
Friday Morning
July 10, 1840

At dawn the next morning Witherspoon stood with Lottie's arms around him, watching Squire, Drummer and Kentucky, his best friends, mount up to ride south.

"This won't take too long, Jeb. Don't worry! I promise, we'll be back."

Witherspoon reached out, shook Squire's hand. "Hurry back, pard'ner."

When the three were well beyond the livery stables, heading south out of Brisbie, Witherspoon sighed. He kicked a pebble down Main Street, then, turning to Lottie he said, "Lottie, let's you'n me go home. I think we can take two, three days at least; catch up on gettin' to know each other, an' thet ranch of ours."

"Sounds good, Ranger. I'll make your favorite potato salad, and we can have a picnic down on the Little Red."

"Yeah. An' I just got paid, so's I can practice tossin' silver down yore blouse."

"There you go again, Jeb Witherspoon! Is that all you can think of? I wasn't even thinkin' about silver -- or blouses for that matter. Who needs blouses or silver? We're going skinny dippin', right after the potato salad!"

"Lottie Witherspoon!"

"Yes, Honey?"

"Who needs potato salad?"

They rode in silence for a few minutes, a thing quite unfamiliar to Jeb. Then finally,

"Jeb, Honey?"

"Yes, my darlin'?

"How do you like the name, Frederick?"

"Now, who the hell is Frederick?"

"Could be your firstborn son, Jacob."

"My firstbo.....?   -- Lottie Witherspoon!" Jeb gasped. "Are you shore?"

"Course, I'm shore," Lottie giggled. "Helluva day ain't it, Sweetie?" she proposed, philosophically.

And on they rode.

The End

A Lad From Sardinia The Adventures of Morgan Harmony
(YA / Christian)

The year is 1622. Morgan Harmony, along with his young brother and their Aunt Harmy, boards a square-rigged warship, captained by his great uncle, Willum. The ship is commissioned by the High Courts of Spain to rid the Mediterranean Sea of pirates, to make the Med safe for commercial trade, and to aid any in need on the waters.

The Age of Sail comes alive as every day brings new adventures, dangers, new lessons to learn, and more maturity.

Aunt Harmy gathers the crew for Christian teachings, while the captain and other ship's officers teach the young lad skills and attributes to serve him well as he grows into manhood.

Miss Roseanna Lynn, a lass pulled from the sea, becomes Morgan's compelling and close friend; together they become adept in the ways of the sea . . . and love. The story is a page-turner from start to finish with just the right mix of adventure, pirates, romance, ethics and humor ... and it is completely set in verse!

Current pricing on my website: www·ferdigwerks·com

Poetpourri A Labyrinth Of Wandering Thought
(short stories & poetry)

A delightful variety of Poems, Prose Poetry,
Vignettes and Short Stories to inspire, encourage and
brighten your life. From children's fairy tales, fables, and
tall tales - to warm, satisfying stories of encouragement,
love, and
completeness. Written in a style akin to an admixture
of Robert Service and Rudyard Kipling . . .
with just a pinch of Shel Silverstein -

From Joe DeCenzo - Author, Past Poet Laureate --
Sunland--Tujunga, CA:
"First off, the primary font you've selected is -- a joy to
read -- easy and comfortable. It was like being served a warm
slice of Americana fresh off the window sill before the
neighborhood hooligans could swipe it for themselves. You
evoked memories that I think cross over a generation or two.
Although growing up is different now than it was for you and me,
I think many people can still relate to your vignettes. I particularly
liked "Perhaps, Perhaps Not!", "Sweatin' Bullets", "Up Near
Fredricksburg", and "The Sentinel". I loved the use of vernacular
and the way you ended with "Timeless" -- a very meaningful way
to end the book."

Current pricing on my website: www·ferdigwerks·com

Cowboy Justice -- On The Border --

Contemporary Crime Novel. The account of Frank Justice, a Nogales Homicide Detective, whose 160 acre property near the village of Elgin is a favorite point of entry for human traffickers, drug smugglars, and other illegals crossing into Arizona from Mexico. It seems Federal efforts are no match for the hordes marching north.

Finally, after much frustration, the governor sanctions a task force -- a team but with one purpose: protect the border where those Coyotes and their "Cargo" abounds.

A governor's recruiter offers Frank Justice a part in this vigilante endeavor, It takes little effort . . . besides, she's smart, beautiful, and she likes fast cars.

Current pricing on my website: www·ferdigwerks·com

A Cry for Justice -- sequel crime story --

Continuing Crime Novel with Frank Justice, a hardened Arizona cop, turned vigilante. He loves this country, especially his ranch on the Arizona border, but he's sickened by the flood of illegals coming into the United Stats and never leaving, or returning again and again, committing crimes with impunity. So, with a little help, he's been putting a dent in cartel activity - trafficking and drug smuggling efforts flowing across the border, especially those using his beloved ranch, Thistledew, as a conduit for such activities.

His efforts and abilities have traveled to other states. Now east coast governors are clamoring for his help in their states . . . .Frank finds himself a wanted man, some for his expertise, some for his head, and not in a nice way.

Current pricing on my website: *www·ferdigwerks·com*